Also by Pa

SERVANT OF THE CROWN, HEIR TO THE CROWN: BOOK ONE

After tragedy changes the course of his life, he serves as a soldier for years until a single act of self-sacrifice thrusts his future into the world of politics.

Banished with little more than the clothes on his back, he seeks a new purpose, for what is a warrior who has nothing left to fight for?

A fateful meeting with another lost soul unmasks a shocking secret, compelling him to take up the mantle of guardian. Bandits, the Black Hand, and even the king, he battles them all for the future of the realm.

∾

SWORD OF THE CROWN, HEIR TO THE CROWN: BOOK TWO

When an invading army crosses the Mercerian border, the only thing standing between victory and defeat is an heir to the crown with no battle experience.

Enter Dame Beverly Fitzwilliam, who has trained for this moment since she first held a sword. From her relentless pursuit of knighthood to the day she single-handedly saves the king's life and earns her spurs, she has searched for someone worthy of her fealty.

Her destiny will be determined in a monumental clash of forces where success can save the kingdom, but failure can only mean certain death.

∾

HEART OF THE CROWN, HEIR TO THE CROWN: BOOK THREE

For as long as he can remember, Alric dreamed of being a hero; of defeating a dragon and saving the princess, but his royal position would never allow it, until…

The arrival of the Mercerian Emissaries demands a princely escort, and his tranquil life is upended from the beginning, as havoc seems to follow these dignitaries everywhere.

From fighting unknown creatures to defending the life of a royal, he discovers that becoming a hero is much more dangerous than he ever imagined. No matter what the outcome, his life will never be the same.

MERCERIAN TALES:

Stories of the Past

PAUL J BENNETT

Dedication

For my daughters, Christie, Stephanie and Amanda.

May you always level up with ease.

Prologue

BODDEN

Summer 960 MC*
(*Mercerian Calendar)

The wood in the fireplace crackled as Gerald Matheson dropped another log onto the embers. Pausing a moment to watch the ensuing blaze erupt, he returned to the comfort of his chair, satisfied in the knowledge that the room would soon heat up. Princess Anna lay on the floor with her feet to the fire while her back was comforted by the body of her massive hound, Tempus. As she waited for the warmth to curl around her, her body was snuggled into a blanket to ward off the evening's chill.

Baron Richard Fitzwilliam reclined nearby, sipping wine from a tankard while his daughter, Beverly, sat oiling her sword. Dame Hayley Chambers, the recently knighted King's Ranger, was chatting with her quietly, as the fire sparked back to life.

"It's almost like old times, Gerald," commented Fitz.

Gerald smiled, "Not quite, my lord; we've all gotten a little older."

A small laugh escaped the princess, "Not all of us are old, Gerald."

"Are you sure," said Fitz, before Gerald could respond to the princess's good-natured banter, "that you don't want me to accompany you to Westland, Highness? The Knights of Bodden would be only too happy to act as your escort."

"No, Baron. Much as I appreciate the offer, you're needed here to protect the border. I don't want to come back to Merceria, only to find it overrun. Besides, I've got Beverly and Hayley here, along with my other new knights; I'll be safe enough."

The room quieted, and then Beverly put down her sword. "Remember when you used to tell me stories in front of the fire, Father?"

Anna, who only a moment ago was laying tranquilly on her beloved pet, perked up. "Stories? Do tell."

"Baron Fitzwilliam used to tell all manner of stories to young Lady Beverly. She loved them," explained Gerald.

"I love stories, too," a now animated Anna, gushed. "Would you be willing to regale us with one, Baron?"

"Well," said Fitz, as he absently stroked his beard, "what kind of stories do you like?"

Anna sat up, turning to face the others with a sparkle in her eye. Even Tempus' ears picked up. "I like all kinds of stories."

"You realize," said Gerald, "once you start, there's no stopping. You'll be telling stories all night long."

"What if we took turns?" suggested Beverly.

"Oooh, even better," begged Anna.

"I'm afraid I don't remember any of the stories I used to tell Beverly. It's been many years since we had a young girl in the Keep," responded the baron.

"How about when you first encountered Albreda?" asked Beverly. "I've often wondered how you two met each other. I understand it was some time ago."

"Now, that," said Fitz, getting into the spirit of it, "is an interesting story, an interesting story indeed. It all started back in '33 when I was still a young man..."

Fitz and the Witch: Part I

THE THING IN THE WOODS

Spring 933 MC

L ord Richard Fitzwilliam stepped forward, sizing up his opponent carefully, shield ready, should he need it. In front of him, his sparring partner waited, shifting his feet as he so often did. They had gone through this countless times before; the man was quite capable of predicting Fitz's moves, and the lord struggled to think of a tactic that might catch him off guard. Finally, he settled on a straightforward attack, striking with a stabbing motion, his sword easily blocked by a shield.

"You'll have to do better than that, Lord," the man said.

"You're positively chatty today, Gerald, let's see how you handle my shield." His line spoken, he stepped forward, using the rim of his shield to drive his opponent back. Fitz was fast, but Sergeant Gerald Matheson was faster. He pivoted on his feet and countered with his own shield, striking that of his attacker, rim to rim, sending a shock up the lord's arm.

"That's a good counter, my friend," said Lord Richard.

"It better be, Lord, I learned it from you."

"You know, my dear fellow, it amazes me how quickly you pick things up."

"I constantly practice, Lord," explained Gerald.

"I've watched you. You know, you really should slow down a little, enjoy life a bit more." As soon as he finished his words, he realized his mistake, for his friend was still mourning the loss of his family last autumn.

"There's little to enjoy, Lord. I want only to kill Norlanders."

It was hard for Fitz to see him in such anguish. Gerald had become obsessed, training whenever he wasn't on duty. He knew the man was burying himself in his work, losing his humanity; soon even the remnants of his friend would be burned away by his pursuit of revenge. It was at this precise moment that inspiration hit him.

"I have a job for you, Gerald," Lord Richard proclaimed. "I want you to lead a patrol."

The young warrior eased his stance to stare at Fitz in disbelief, "Me, Lord?"

"Yes, Gerald, you. There's little else I can teach you about fighting, but plenty more for you to learn about leading men. I think the experience would do you good."

Gerald was a plain-spoken man, not one to brag about his achievements. This unexpected praise left him staring back in discomfort, unsure how to respond.

"Well?" prompted Fitz. "What do you think?"

"What do I think?"

"Yes, man. Would you like to lead a patrol?"

"You're asking me? Shouldn't you just command me?"

Lord Richard looked at him with compassion, "No, Gerald, I'm asking you. Do you think you're ready?"

"Aye, Lord," his sparring partner replied, though to Fitz's mind, the man was less than enthusiastic.

"Very well, then. You're a Sergeant, so I order you to take out a patrol. Take the route to the Greene farm, you know the way, we've been there often enough."

"Aye, Lord," said Gerald, straightening visibly.

At this moment one of the older knights, Sir James, entered the courtyard. "Your Lordship?" he enquired.

"Yes, Sir James?" acknowledged Fitz.

"The baron wants to see you in the map room."

"Very well," replied Lord Richard, "tell him I'm on the way." He turned back to his sparring partner, "It seems this practice is over, my friend, I have been summoned by my brother. Best if I don't keep him waiting, and you need to be on your way if you want to be back before dark."

"Aye, Lord," grumbled Gerald before heading off to the stables.

Fitz hoped leading a patrol would bring the man out of his self-imposed exile. Since the death of his family, Gerald had become withdrawn and solitary; perhaps forcing him to look after a patrol was just the thing he needed to bring him out of his grief.

He was still musing on this very idea as his feet carried him toward the map room, up the spiral staircase to the highest room in Bodden Keep.

Baron Edward Fitzwilliam stood at the map table, a large map of the barony spread out before him. Sir James stood to his left, while Sir Rodney was to his right, his large nose buried in a handkerchief. As Lord Richard entered the room, the knight let out an earth-shattering sneeze. The sound startled all within the room as it echoed through the chamber.

"You should get that looked at, Sir Rodney," the baron chided.

"Sorry, my lord," the knight turned bright crimson as he apologized.

"You might try some hot cider," suggested Lord Richard as he entered. "My sergeant tells me it does wonders."

Baron Edward eyed him with a look of annoyance, "Perhaps now that my brother has deigned to present himself, we can now get down to business?"

"Of course, Brother," Lord Richard replied.

Edward cleared his throat, then began, "As you are no doubt aware, raiders from Norland have been particularly active of late. In the past few months, they have attacked five of our farms, stealing what they can, and burning the rest. I needn't tell you our stocks of food are dangerously low, leaving us no choice but to resort to hunting in order to make up the shortfall."

Edward stabbed down with his finger. "This," he continued, "is the Whitewood, as you all know. It lies just to our northeast and has an abundant source of game, but of late our hunters have come under increasingly dangerous attacks from the creatures that dwell therein."

"You mean the animals?" asked a surprised Lord Richard.

Edward gave his brother another look of annoyance, "Yes, I mean animals. Something is agitating them, making them more aggressive."

"Are you trying to tell me," said Lord Richard with a grin, "that the squirrels are attacking?"

"This is no laughing matter, Richard. Men have died."

This new information immediately sobered Lord Richard. He didn't pay much attention to the affairs of the barony; his job was to command the soldiers stationed here. "I'm sorry, Brother, I had no idea."

"Perhaps," said the baron irritably, "if you paid more attention to what is happening around you, instead of spending all day exercising your sword arm, you would have known about this."

Fitz nodded his agreement and did his best to look contrite. "You were saying?"

"Attacks have been on the rise lately," the baron continued, "and seem to be coordinated."

They all fell silent at the thought. It was Sir Rodney that spoke first, "Are you suggesting, Lord, that some type of creature is commanding them?"

"Possibly," said the baron, "and I've already arranged for help, a King's Ranger."

The knights nodded their agreement; the King's Rangers are known as expert trackers. One of them must surely be familiar with the Whitewood.

"May I make a suggestion?" put forth Lord Richard.

"By all means, Brother."

"Perhaps an escort, to keep the ranger protected if he should need it. There may still be Norlanders in the area."

"For once, I agree with you," said the baron. "I want you to take Sir Rodney and Sir James with you, along with four new knights."

Lord Richard frowned, "New knights?"

"Yes, Brother, they just came in this morning. All from the finest families, I'm told."

Lord Richard noticed the look of mirth on his brother's face; breaking in new knights was his least favourite pastime. "Just a moment, Lord," he said as he rushed to the window.

He looked to the west, but Gerald was just disappearing over the far hill as he watched; too late to recall him. He would have liked to have his sergeant with him to help handle the knights. "Damn," he swore.

The baron, misinterpreting his curse, exploded, "I've had enough of this attitude of yours, Richard. When are you going to take life seriously? I am the baron, and as my brother, you are the heir. If I were to die, you would be responsible for all of this," he said, pointing at the map to emphasize his point.

Fitz turned suddenly at the outburst, surprised by the venom in his brother's voice. "I'm sorry, I wasn't upset over that, I had something else in mind. I-"

"Get going," the baron interrupted, "you'll need to ride out as soon as possible. The ranger is staying at the Blue Swallow, you can meet him there and then ride out together. I'll send word that you're coming. Make sure you get to the bottom of this, Richard."

"Aye, Lord." Fitz immediately obeyed, for knowing his brother well, he recognized he would brook no further discussion on the matter. He could see the strain of authority was not sitting well on Edward's shoulders and, truth be told, Fitz didn't envy his brother's position; being the baron of a remote location like Bodden would be a difficult task.

After assembling in the courtyard, they rode into the village to find the ranger. Lord Richard took the lead, with Sir Rodney riding beside him, his nose once again, buried in a handkerchief. The fresh faces of the new knights followed in pairs with Sir James bringing up the rear.

An explosive sneeze erupted from Sir Rodney, and Fitz looked at him in sympathy, "Did you try some hot cider?"

"No, my lord, there wasn't time."

"Perhaps you should consider sitting this one out?"

"No, Lord, I can't leave you with this lot," he jabbed his thumb behind him. "Even with Sir James, they're likely to be a handful."

"This may surprise you, Rodney, but I've dealt with their type before," as he said this, he witnessed a fallen look cross the older knight's face, so he quickly added, "but I appreciate your presence. Tell me, what do you know about them?"

Sir Rodney finished wiping his nose and tucked his handkerchief away as he answered, "They all come from wealthy families, Lord."

"That's no surprise. Show me a knight that doesn't."

"Perhaps I should say wealthier than most? Sir Lionel there has a reputation for duelling. He earned that scar across his nose in Wincaster."

"I suppose that at least means the man knows how to fight," Fitz mused.

"Aye, my lord, but he lacks discipline. I fear it will take a lot of work to break him in."

Lord Richard glanced over his shoulder at the horsemen following, "I'll keep that in mind. What about the rest?"

"The shorter one is Sir Dudley, probably the strongest of the group, and the quietest. He doesn't talk much. I suspect he'll fit in rather easily. The tall, thin man is Sir Ethan; his father serves on the King's Council. We'll have to mind our manners around him; his family's got some pull." Sir Rodney let out a sudden sneeze and reached again for his handkerchief, "Sorry, my lord."

Fitz waited for the man to finish before he spoke, "And the last one? The one with the neatly trimmed beard?"

"That," said Sir Rodney, "is Sir Maynard. He's the most outspoken of the group, and I would say their unofficial leader."

"Leader? Are you saying we're going to have to break up this little band?"

"I suppose that depends," mused Sir Rodney.

"Depends on what?"

"On how they do on this expedition, Lord."

Lord Richard looked at the old knight and smiled, "That will be your job, Rodney. I hope you're up to it."

The man stiffened in his saddle, "Of course, Lord, I won't let a little thing like a cold get in the way."

"Glad to hear it," Fitz responded, grateful to have an ally on this patrol, even if it wasn't Gerald.

They pulled up in front of the Blue Swallow to see a rough looking man astride a weather-beaten horse, his dark green cloak thrown back, revealing the glint of chainmail beneath.

"Lord Richard, I presume," the man remarked. "I'm Brock Dayton, King's Ranger."

Fitz pulled his horse up beside Dayton and extended his hand. "Glad to meet you, though I must admit to being a little surprised to see a King's Ranger this far north."

Dayton grasped the proffered hand with a firm grip. "I heard reports of some trouble with wild animals from a merchant I met on the road, so I thought I would investigate. The baron heard of my arrival and sent word to me. You must be the baron's brother?"

"Yes, Lord Richard Fitzwilliam, but you may call me Fitz."

"Nobody ever does," piped up Sir Rodney.

Fitz turned in his saddle, "What was that?"

"Nothing, Lord," the knight said as he fumbled in vain to suppress another sneeze.

"Where would you like to begin, Lord?" asked the ranger.

"We'll ride to the edge of the Whitewood, and we'll show you where the last attack occurred. After that, it's up to you. You're the expert in these matters."

"Very well," said Brock, "lead on."

They made their way out of the little village past the wall that was under construction. The houses were grouped around the Keep, with a new wall being constructed to give the village some protection, but it was an ongoing affair, and Lord Richard feared it might never be complete.

Soon, they were past the half-built wall and making their way across the fields, the Keep shrinking behind them.

"Tell me, Brock," said Fitz, "how did you become a King's Ranger?"

The man mulled over the question before answering, "I was always a hunter, Lord. While I lived in Shrewesdale, I was hired to help with one of the earl's hunts."

"I hear," Sir Rodney interjected, "the earl's hunts are quite extravagant."

"It's true," confirmed the ranger, "though that only extends to his friends. The rest of us were far too busy. The hunt was led by a ranger named Madson."

"I take it," said Fitz, "that's how you became a ranger?"

"Aye, Lord, he saw something in me and convinced me to join the King's Rangers. That was five years ago."

"And how is life as a ranger?" asked Fitz.

"Hard work," the man replied, "but rewarding."

Closing the range on their destination, the small group could now make out the edge of the woods that was their target.

"Up here is where the last attack occurred, Lord," said Sir Rodney. "A hunting party was just leaving, by that large tree over there, the one with the twisted trunk."

They rode forward, coming to a halt just shy of the undergrowth that marked the edge of the Whitewood.

"I see how it gets its name," said the ranger, looking at the cluster of birch trees. "Is the entire forest like that?"

"No," answered Lord Richard, "but those are quite common here."

Dismounting, they lead the horses toward the large tree. Sir James ordered the new knights to guard the horses as Sir Rodney guided Lord Richard and the ranger to the site of the last attack.

"It was right over here," pointed the older knight. "A hunting party was coming out of the woods with a deer they'd killed. You can still see evidence of the attack where the underbrush has been trampled down."

Brock began examining the ground carefully. "Tell me more," he asked. "What was the nature of the attack?"

"The hunters heard the baying of wolves and were rushing back to the edge of the wood when a bear came at them."

"A bear? Are you sure?" asked Brock.

"Oh yes," replied Sir Rodney. "There were survivors, and their wounds definitely looked like those from bear claws."

"Most unusual," muttered the ranger. "And they're sure it was wolves?"

"Yes, why?" asked the knight.

"It's most unusual," said Brock, "for wolves and bears to work together. I've certainly never heard of it before."

It was Fitz who spoke next, "Do you think something is behind this?"

"Hard to say," the man responded, "but I suspect so. Let me see what I can discover from the site of the attack. Keep your men out of the way so they don't ruin the tracks."

Fitz wandered back to the horses. Sir Maynard was helping himself to a wineskin that hung from his saddle while Sir Lionel was talking to him. As

Lord Richard approached, the two grew silent, both staring at him. Was there a guilty look on their faces? Fitz wasn't sure if he was imagining things.

"We're waiting on the ranger," he explained. "In the meantime, keep your eyes peeled. Remember, there are wild animals around here, creatures quite capable of killing you if you're inattentive."

They nodded their affirmation, but Fitz felt uneasy. This was no simple military exercise, and he didn't know what to expect. He watched, absently, as the ranger stooped to examine the ground. Hearing the snap of a twig, he looked to his side to see Sir James approaching. The man stood beside him a moment, watching Brock at work.

"Do you trust him, Lord?" the knight asked.

Fitz was surprised by his question. "Trust him? Why wouldn't I trust him?"

"He's a King's Ranger, Lord. They've become a law unto themselves."

"Don't be ridiculous, man; he serves the king. Besides, he's the only one around here that knows how to track, unless you have a better suggestion?"

"No, my lord," the man retorted, and then fell silent.

It was only a little while later that the ranger called them to follow. The trail led deeper into the woods, and the group followed, walking beside their horses. The ground here was very uneven with fallen branches and leaves often covering holes that could damage an ankle or foot. The group made their way forward, steadily, until Fitz thought it likely near noon. At the ranger's suggestion, they halted for a rest. Fitz pulled his wineskin and took a deep drink. The air here was still, and moisture seemed to cling to their skin until it ran down in rivulets.

Shortly after resuming their trek, the ranger was stopping them again as he knelt to examine the ground in detail. "There's something here," he said, beckoning to Lord Richard.

"What is it?" Fitz replied, his interest sparked.

"There's a footprint," the man explained.

"There's a surprise," inserted Sir Maynard snidely, "a footprint where people have been hunting."

"Shut up," spat Sir Rodney, "and let the tracker have his say."

"Please continue," urged Lord Richard.

"As I was saying," the man continued, "there's a footprint here, but it looks a little strange."

"In what way?" asked Fitz.

"It appears to be a Human print, encased in a boot of some type."

"A boot of some type? What do you mean?"

"Well, it's obviously covered, likely with leather, but there's no evidence of stitching or nails. I've never seen its like before."

"How do you know it's Human?"

"Oh, you can see the markings where the balls of the feet strike, it's definitely Human, but there's more, there are wolf prints nearby. Whoever it is, is being followed."

He looked at Fitz as the meaning sunk in. Being the baron's brother, it was his duty to safeguard the people of Bodden. They must hasten to rescue whoever was in danger.

"We must hurry then," said Fitz. "Can you tell how old the tracks are?"

"The tracks I was following earlier are older, while these are more recent. I reckon we're only a short distance away."

"How short a distance?" queried Lord Richard. "Can we catch up before nightfall?"

The ranger stood, "Oh, we'll catch them long before then. In fact, I'm surprised we can't hear something in the distance. I suggest we draw weapons; those wolves must be close."

Fitz turned to Sir Rodney, but his unofficial second was already giving the order, and a moment later everybody stood with their swords held ready in their hands.

Leaving Sir Dudley to care for the horses, they moved ahead in single file, following the lead of the ranger. They had only gone an the flight of an arrow when the ranger halted and crouched, the rest automatically mimicking his actions to the best of their abilities, being as they were clad in chainmail. The green attired tracker motioned with his hand for Fitz and Sir Rodney to creep up to his position in a crouched posture, hoping to avoid detection. The ranger waited until the two came beside him and slowly used the edge of his sword to part the leaves of a fallen branch before him.

They looked into a small clearing where a woman stood, her back to them. She was tall and thin, and though they couldn't see her face, they observed her long black hair that was braided, falling down her back. She was wearing a plain green dress that went to the ground, the hem torn and dirty from travelling through the woods. Fitz, about to stand and announce himself, was stayed the ranger's hand on his forearm warning him to stop. The lord looked down at the tracker who pointed to the side of the clearing. Soon, Fitz realized what he meant, for a group of wolves were at the edge of the tree line, looking in the woman's direction.

Lord Richard had fought for years against Norlanders, but here, in this clearing, he was out of his element. Were they Human, he would simply attack, but the woman's life was in jeopardy; if the knights charged, there was no guarantee that they would reach her before the wolves sprung.

The ranger leaned in close to Lord Richard's ear to whisper, "I'll hold them off with arrows, you must reach her as quickly as possible."

Fitz nodded his understanding and waved his men forward. Brock moved closer to a tree so that the growth would hide him as he strung his bow. A moment later, his arrow notched, he nodded, and the knights sprang from their cover, dashing towards the woman. It only took a moment for the woman to react, for chainmail is noisy and, combined with the slapping of scabbards and the thud of many boots, it drew her attention quickly. She turned at the sound, her eyes going wild as the group burst out of the cover of the trees.

An arrow buried itself into one of the wolves, releasing a terrified howl from the creature. The woman screamed as Fitz raced toward her. He shouted a warning, but the clanking of his armour and yelling of the knights drowned out his voice. He wheeled as he reached her, facing the threat from the edge of the woods, protecting her from the expected onslaught of wild beasts.

He saw a blur to his left, and suddenly Sir James was struggling with a wolf on his back. Sir Rodney swung at the creature, and it leaped away, growling as it did so. The whole clearing had erupted into a cacophony as the low growls melded with the clank of armour to produce an almost melancholy sound. Fitz turned abruptly as one of the beasts surged toward him, instinctively blocking. The creature swerved at the last moment and ran past him, his movements too slow to do anything but watch in amazement. He got a quick glimpse of Sir Ethan, a wolf tugging at his leg, but the beast's teeth failed to penetrate the man's chainmail leggings. It was almost comical to Fitz's eyes, had it not been a matter of life and death. The tall knight swung with his sword, and a yelp indicated a hit, forcing the creature to release its grasp.

All around him, dark shapes flew past as more and more wolves materialized. Arrow followed arrow, flying into the clearing, the deadly shafts striking true more often than not. Throughout the barrage, the knights had formed a protective circle around the woman, who was now screaming, but he couldn't make out her words in the ensuing pandemonium. A wolf bit into Fitz's arm, his mail protecting his flesh. He flung his attacker off, its teeth gliding from his mail without penetrating.

Suddenly, out of the corner of his eyes, he saw a massive shape bearing down on the ranger. He yelled out a warning, but the archer was too occupied with the multitude of targets within his view. Unable to do anything but watch in horror, Fitz bore witness to the great bear striking out. A terrible shriek of pain pierced the woods as the creature's claws dug into their intended victim. The animal disappeared into the woods with his prey, the ranger's screams trailing off as the great beast did who knew what to the poor man.

Sir Rodney ducked as a wolf jumped at him, flying over his head, an arrow protruding from its flank. The knight twisted and struck with his sword, covering himself in the blood that spurted from the beast. Fitz stepped forward to finish the creature off, but as he raised his sword, the woman screamed.

"NO," she roared, "Enough! Flee for your lives!"

Astonished by her actions, he looked to her, confident she had been talking to them, but to his surprise, she was leaning over an injured wolf, its blood staining her hand as she stroked its fur. The creature lurched to its feet and ran off into the underbrush, disappearing from sight. Soon, the clearing was quiet, save for the heavy breathing of the two-legged combatants. They were all standing around, looking confused by the unexpected development. The woman faced him, her hands held out in front of her, waiting for something.

"I surrender," she offered, "but you must stop the killing."

"Tell that to the animals," said Sir Maynard, in a harsh tone.

"They were trying to protect me," she retorted, "doing what they thought best."

Lord Richard could only stare at her as her words sank in. "You're behind the attacks," he declared. "Why would you order them to attack?"

"You invaded their land, what did you expect."

Sir James was, by now, standing where the ranger lay, but he emerged from behind the tree, his face pale. "He's dead, I'm afraid, ripped to pieces."

"She's killed a King's Ranger," said Sir Maynard, "that's the death penalty. We need to put her to death."

"Quiet," commanded Fitz. "We need to take her back to Bodden."

"Are you insane?" Sir Maynard continued. "She's dangerous; she could summon another attack. She's a witch."

"Then we bind her and gag her," Fitz retorted. "Sir Rodney, prepare the prisoner. We'll take her back with us."

"What of the ranger, Lord?" enquired Sir James.

"We'll bring his body back with us so we can see to a proper burial."

"But Lord-" objected Sir Maynard.

"Enough!" yelled Fitz. "My brother placed me in command, I'll not have you question my authority. Now," he paused to calm his temper, "we need to get moving, or it'll be dark before we get back to the Keep."

Sir Dudley was called over with the horses, and he began the process of wrapping up the ranger's body. The woman watched them intently as Sir Rodney tied her hands. Fitz wondered who she was, but was too busy directing the others to begin any interrogation.

Sometime later they were on their way back to the Keep. Lord Richard and Sir Rodney took the lead, with Sir Maynard and Sir Lionel following directly behind. The prisoner was tethered to Sir Maynard's horse by a rope which ran from his saddle to her hands that were bound securely. Sir Dudley and Sir Ethan rode behind her, eyes darting about in case the creatures returned to finish what they started. Sir James brought up the rear, leading a horse with the ranger's body slung over the saddle.

"What do you make of it, Lord?" asked Sir Rodney, his cold all but forgotten.

"It's most curious," said Fitz. "I've never heard tell of anything like it."

Sir Rodney turned in the saddle to look at the prisoner, struggling to keep up. "Isn't it dangerous, trying to hold a witch?"

Fitz likewise turned to view the woman, "She doesn't look very dangerous now. Anyway, it's for my brother to decide, he's the baron."

He was about to turn back, but the woman stumbled as Sir Maynard tugged abruptly on her line. She fell, and the knight, laughing, sped up his horse slightly, dragging her painfully along the uneven ground.

"Enough of that," said Fitz, irritated at the young knight's actions. "Let her get to her feet. It'll do no good to bring her back dead."

Sir Maynard halted, dismounting to drag the woman to her feet. "You're a pretty one," he said, almost spitting in her face, "I bet I could break you."

"I said that's enough!" roared Lord Richard.

Sir Rodney had turned his horse and now rode up to the younger knight. In a flash, the older knight's sword was at Sir Maynard's throat. "You were given an order," he said, "or do you choose to dishonour your oath?"

There was a tense moment as the two men stared at each other, then the younger man cast his eyes to the ground, "No, Sir Rodney. My apologies. I was just overcome by the death of the ranger."

"Understandable," said Sir Rodney, "but we must still carry out our duty."

"I wonder," said Fitz, "if we might make better progress by putting the woman on the ranger's horse?" He rode over to look down on their prisoner. "Can you ride?" he asked.

She nodded her head.

"Very well, let's put her on the horse, and just to make sure there are no further improprieties, she'll ride beside me."

"Is that wise, Lord," pressed Sir Rodney.

"You take the lead, Rodney, and we'll keep a man to either side of us in the event she tries to make a break for it. Just in case, we'll keep her hands bound and tie them to my horse. Will that suffice?"

The elder knight nodded, "Indeed, Lord. I should think those precautions would be entirely adequate."

Rodney settled the prisoner on the ranger's horse, in front of his body. The sky was starting to darken with clouds, and they would be lucky to arrive before the rain came. The ride continued in silence until the Keep was in view, then Fitz turned to the prisoner, pulling the gag from her mouth. "You haven't told us your name," he said. "What shall we call you?"

"It matters not," she replied. "I am your prisoner, and I expect no mercy from you. Call me what you like."

Riding on, he let her words sink in. Who was this woman, and how did she control the animals. Was she indeed a witch? He knew little of them. They were said to be the masters of nature, what one would call an Earth Mage, but his knowledge of the arcane arts was very limited.

Fitz considered himself a well-read man, but magic had been in decline for generations, and now there was only one mage left in Merceria, the King's Healer, Andronicus. Could there be other mages that the crown didn't know about? He thought it unlikely, but in truth, it wasn't his place to worry about it; that was the prerogative of his brother, the rightful Baron of Bodden.

"What will the baron do with her?" piped up Sir James, who was just behind them.

"I know what I'd like to do with her," said Sir Maynard. "There's only one way to break a woman!"

Fitz turned in his saddle, ready to explode in rage at the man's tone, but Sir James had spurred his horse forward, and struck the younger man, sending him to the ground. "I've had enough of your disrespect for Lord Richard, you ungrateful cur. I don't know what they teach you in Wincaster these days, but here we respect the chain of command."

The young knight got to his feet and stared daggers at Sir James.

"Mount up," said Sir James, "and I'll have no more of this talk."

The earlier silence descended once more while the sullen group rode through the village. Soon, they passed the gates and headed straight toward the stables.

"I'll take care of disciplining him," offered Sir James, "even if I have to beat some sense into him myself."

Lord Richard and Sir Rodney escorted the prisoner to the great hall where Baron Edward awaited them.

"Is she the cause of the attacks?" Baron Edward asked, without preamble.

"Yes, Brother, at least we think so."

"And how did she accomplish this?" the baron demanded.

"She is a witch," blurted out Sir Rodney.

"A witch? I suppose that would explain things." Baron Edward stepped forward, holding up her chin with his hand, "What is your name, witch?"

Her look of defiance was visible to all. "You caused this," she spat out, "by your attacks on the Whitewood."

Edward smiled, "You're my prisoner now, I suggest you conduct yourself in an appropriate manner." He looked to his younger brother, "It would have been better if you had killed her," he suggested, "and spared us the trouble of locking her up."

"She surrendered herself," Fitz protested. "What was I supposed to do?"

Edward gave him a look that told him what he thought of the situation. "So, witch, what shall we do with you, eh?"

The woman spat on the ground, "That's what I think of you, Baron."

"Take her to the dungeons, Sir Rodney. Perhaps after she's had some time to rot in the darkness, she'll reconsider her attitude."

The knight led her away while Fitz remained to talk to his elder brother, but it was Edward that spoke first.

"I don't like this," he stated. "Having a witch locked up here could be dangerous. You should have killed her; it would have made it easier for everyone."

"We have to determine what is happening here, Edward. Find out why this war started."

"War? This isn't a war. It's a witch that's been ordering some attacks."

"Perhaps we can reason with her?"

"Reason? She killed a King's Ranger; there can be no reasoning with that, the woman is insane."

"Still," offered Fitz, "we're at an impasse. I would like to try and resolve this. The animals are still out there, and our men are not safe."

"By all means," replied the baron, "but she stays in the dungeon until I say otherwise."

Lord Richard left the hall, his mind in turmoil. Who was this woman and why did she feel compelled to protect the Whitewood? Was there some secret held within the forest that she was defending?

-Interlude I-

BODDEN

Summer 960 MC

"And that," offered Fitz, "was the first time I met Albreda."

The others sat in stunned silence for a few moments.

"Fascinating," Anna was the first to break the silence. "I would never have dreamed it."

"I'm a little confused," added Dame Beverly. "Are you saying you took her prisoner?"

"Well, my dear, that's rather obvious, isn't it?" said Fitz.

"Yes, but she told me she owed you a favour. How can she owe you a favour if you captured her?"

"Well, there's more to this story, but I believe it's time for some wine. Gerald, be a friend and pass me the Hawksburg red, will you?"

Gerald strode over to the side table to retrieve the bottle, pouring the baron some wine. "I don't remember you bringing a prisoner in," he mused. "When did you say this was?"

"Back in '33," said Fitz. "You led your first patrol, do you remember?"

"Aye, I remember my first patrol, but I still don't remember the prisoner."

"That's because my brother, in his infinite wisdom, ordered no one to speak of it."

"Isn't that rather strange?" piped up Hayley. "Was your brother always so secretive, Lord?"

"My brother was a headstrong individual," he replied, "but the thought of a witch in the Keep was, perhaps, too much for him to handle."

"Do you think he went mad?" asked Beverly.

"Not mad, but he was angry, certainly. When our father died, Edward was thrust into the title rather suddenly. He found the responsibility to be quite burdensome."

"But you've handled it well," observed Anna.

"It was quite an adjustment," replied Fitz. "By the time Edward died, I had Gerald here to lean on. I think Edward needed help, but he was always too proud to ask for it."

"I would have liked to have met him," mused Beverly. "I remember the story that Uncle Robert told about how you met Mother. You two seemed to get along well in your younger years."

Baron Fitzwilliam grimaced, "In our younger years, we got along famously. It was only after Edward assumed the mantle of baron that we were more often than not at loggerheads."

"You're avoiding the obvious question," said Anna.

"Which is, Your Highness?"

"What happens next! You told us how you captured Albreda, but that's a long way from explaining how she came to assist us."

"Yes," agreed Hayley. "You've got us on the edge of our seats, you can't stop now."

"Did you seduce her while she was your prisoner?" enquired Anna.

The baron's face turned bright red, "For Saxnor's sake! Of course not, she was my prisoner. I would never dream of such a thing."

"But there must have been some attraction," Anna pressed on.

"No, most definitely not," Fitz exclaimed.

"Well then, tell us the rest of the story," pressed the princess.

Baron Fitzwilliam took a sip of his wine, "Very well. I can see you're not going to stop pestering me until I continue. Now, where was I? Oh yes, it was the spring of 933..."

Fitz and the Witch: Part II

THE PRISONER

Spring 933 MC

The dungeons of Bodden Keep saw little use these days, and as Lord Richard made his way down into them, he held the lantern high, for in these depths there was no light filtering in from above. It was strange to be here, he thought, having played down here as a youngster, typically hiding from his older brother. The dark hallways and small chambers had provided excellent hiding places.

The light from his lantern danced across the walls as he made his way to the cells. When the Keep had been constructed, his ancestor had created a round chamber, some twenty feet across. Branching off from this was eight doorways, one of which was connected to the hallway he now traversed. The others opened into small rooms to hold prisoners, each no more than two paces wide and just deep enough that a grown man could lie flat on the floor. The dungeons were located beneath the barracks, which ensured that even if a prisoner escaped from their cell, there was no viable escape route.

The sound of voices greeted his ears as he entered the circular chamber to see two men sitting at a small wooden table. There were cards laid out, and the guards strained in the dim light to make out what resided in their hands. Light from the flickering torches bounced off the bottle of wine that sat beside them.

At the sound of his approach, one of the men looked up. "My lord," said Sir Maynard, "we hadn't expected to see you here."

"How is it," asked Fitz, "that a knight is here guarding a prisoner? Surely you have better things to do?"

"It was the baron's idea," the man explained. "He felt we should limit who has access to the witch."

The knight's comrade had stood as Lord Richard entered, nodding in respect. With the shadows cast across his face, it wasn't until the man was a hand's reach away that Fitz recognized him.

"Sir Lionel, I see you're eager to lose coins again."

"Lord?" questioned the man.

"You're playing cards with a ruthless gambler. From what I have heard, Sir Maynard here is sure to clean out your purse."

"I still have some tricks up my sleeve, Lord," Sir Lionel replied.

"How's the prisoner been?" asked Fitz.

"Quiet, Lord," said Sir Maynard, "but we've taken efforts to free her tongue."

Lord Richard felt his stomach tighten at the words, "What do you mean, 'efforts'?"

The knight, emboldened by his lord's interest, continued, "The woman has been most uncooperative, Lord, so I came up with a rather original way of dealing with it."

"Which is?" prompted Fitz, struggling to hide the concern in his voice.

Sir Maynard rose to his feet, retrieving the ring of keys from the table beside him, "See for yourself, Lord."

He strode over to the cell and inserted the key into the lock. The door was made of oak, reinforced with metal and Fitz wondered why it was constructed of such material; surely a simple series of bars would have sufficed? The lock made a loud clanking noise as Sir Maynard twisted the key and then swung the door outward. Immediately Fitz was overwhelmed with the stench of urine and filth. The tiny room was enveloped in shadows, and Lord Richard raised his lantern to peer within.

He was repulsed by the sight that greeted him. The ceiling in this cell was some ten feet tall, and in the centre was a metal ring, with two chains hanging from it that ended in manacles. Within these were the arms of the captive, stretched above her head, forcing the prisoner to stand on her toes. She was naked and smeared with dirt, her breath visible in the cold air of the dungeon.

"Without her clothes, she'll soon appreciate a little body warmth," leered Sir Maynard.

Fitz fought hard to control his temper, "What is the meaning of this? Who authorized this treatment?"

Sir Maynard, completely oblivious to the lord's concern, continued, "It was my idea, Lord." He pushed past Lord Richard and ran his hand over the woman's stomach, "We'll put a bastard into her; then she'll talk."

Fitz exploded, punching the man in the chest with the full force of his anger. "How dare you!" he yelled, unable to fully articulate his disgust. "Get out of here!" he ordered. "I'll deal with you later."

Sir Maynard looked ready to object, but as their eyes locked, the knight backed down; striking a man of Lord Richard's status would be a mistake. The man skulked from the room, clutching his stomach.

"Where are her clothes?" Fitz demanded.

Sir Lionel entered the tiny cell. "Here, Lord," he said, handing the rags to Lord Richard.

"Loosen those chains," ordered Fitz, and moved to support the woman's weight. The chains were released, but she was weak and unable to stand. He lowered her, as gently as he could, to the cold stone floor. "I am so sorry," he said, compassion in his voice as he withdrew the pins that held the manacles tightly around her wrists. "I had no idea you were being treated like this."

He handed her the bundle of clothes, and she pulled the dress over her head while he looked away. "What did you expect," she asked, "that I'd be given a comfortable room and politely asked to stop?"

Fitz felt properly chastised. He had indeed thought her imprisonment would be less severe. "I will talk to my brother about this," he promised. "I assure you this treatment will end."

"So I am free to go?" she asked, sarcasm dripping from her tongue.

Fitz turned to look at her. She was straightening her dress and pulling her long black locks from beneath. "I'm afraid that is not within my power, but I can promise you humane treatment while you are a prisoner here."

"How noble of you," she responded, "and how long do you think it will be until you force yourself upon me?"

Fitz was startled. How poorly had the knights treated her that she would think he would harm her? He struggled to respond but ended up merely staring at her in disbelief.

"Don't look so shocked," the woman stated. "I'm familiar with how the nobles of Merceria treat those beneath their station. It's the noble's prerogative to take from those below. Isn't that what they teach young lordlings?"

"I can assure you that is not the way I was raised. While I cannot release you, I will make sure you have decent accommodations while you are a prisoner and that none shall harm you."

"How can you guarantee such a thing? You're not the baron of this Keep."

"I give you my word I shall do all in my power," Fitz said, although he felt they might be empty words. He felt ashamed for the actions of his men, and yet he knew his brother would have condoned such treatment if he had been asked.

"I shall move you to a different part of the dungeon," he offered, "and make sure you at least have a bed to sleep on, and regular meals. I may not be able to release you, but I can ensure you're not mistreated."

"Until your brother decides to have me executed," she spat out.

"I'll go and talk to my brother immediately and straighten this out," he promised. "In the meantime, I will make arrangements to have you moved."

Fitz sought out his brother. As usual, the baron was in the map room, poring over the accounts. He looked up in annoyance as his younger brother entered.

"What brings you here, Brother, finally taking an interest in the accounts?" asked Baron Edward.

"Not today. However, I need to bring something to your attention," said Lord Richard, trying to feel out his brother's mood.

"Oh? Tell me more."

"It's the prisoner," he said, "I'm afraid she's been mistreated."

"That is hardly a concern of mine," the baron responded.

"You can't be serious, Edward. It's imperative that a prisoner, especially a woman, is treated with respect-"

"Or what?" interrupted the baron. "She's a witch, for Saxnor's sake. She deserves everything she gets."

"She's not a witch," Lord Richard exclaimed, defending the woman.

"Yes, she is. She might be called an Earth Mage or a Druid, but she still controls animals. In any book, she'd be described as a witch."

"You cannot allow her to be treated this way," Fitz insisted.

Baron Edward stood, his fury exploding, "I have had it with you. You ride around the land with your fancy horse and knights, while I have to make the difficult decisions. I have a solemn duty to protect the people of Bodden, Richard, and I take that pledge seriously. You think the world runs on honour and duty but it doesn't; it's utter chaos. At any point in time, we are but a moment away from collapse. An inattentive guard could mean the Norlanders are inside the walls of the Keep; a bad storm and our crops could be wiped out. We survive and thrive on hard work and luck. We can't afford to be sentimental!"

"What are you saying? That we should just kill anyone we capture?"

Edward took a deep breath and let it out slowly, "No, Brother. I'm saying you don't have an appreciation for the responsibilities of being the baron. You've always had an easier life, that's no secret. I was the heir. Father made sure I was tending to matters of the barony while you were gallivanting around with your soldiers." His tone softened, "I know it's not your fault, Richard, but you must realize that I am as much a prisoner here as she is."

"Can you at least make sure she is treated with respect?"

The Elder Fitzwilliam looked at his younger brother for some time before finally answering, "Very well, Richard. Since you feel that she has been mistreated, I put you in charge of her."

"What?" Fitz replied.

"You heard me. You will be her jailer. You will be responsible for making sure is supplied with food and water. I will delegate her treatment to you, and to you alone."

"What's the catch," said Fitz. "I know you, Edward. There's always a catch."

"Yes," replied Edward, "there will be conditions."

Fitz nodded knowingly, "And what are these conditions?"

"First," said the baron, "you cannot release her. Secondly, you may tell no one of her imprisonment; you are to be her only visitor. We can't have her using her magic on anyone."

"Very well," Fitz agreed. "I shall trouble you about it no more."

"I doubt that," said the baron, "but for now I will take you at your word. Now get out of here and let me get back to work."

Fitz was pondering his situation when he bumped into his protege, Gerald Matheson. "Gerald, my dear fellow, how did the patrol go?"

"Well, my lord," his sergeant replied. "There's not much going on these days, the Norlanders seem to be quiet of late."

"I wish that was more reassuring," replied Lord Richard, "but I suspect they're up to something big."

"Should we increase the patrols, Lord?"

"Increase the number? No, but perhaps we should strengthen them; a show of force might help dissuade the raiders. I'd like you to double the number of troops you take out."

"Aye, Lord," replied Gerald.

Fitz looked at his friend in thought, "Actually, Gerald, I have a favour to ask."

"A favour, Lord? Of course, what is it?"

"I'd like to send some knights out with you." Fitz held up his hand before the man could object, "I know what you're going to say. You'd have a conflict of command."

"How would I command a knight, Lord? They're above me."

"I'll make it clear to them that they're under your command. If there's any trouble, you report back to me, in person. Clear?"

"Aye, Lord. I don't like it, but I'll do as you wish. Is there anything I need to know?"

"Yes, keep an eye on Sir Maynard, he's one of the new knights. He'll likely cause trouble. I'll send Sir Rodney out with you, to help keep him in line. Rodney will take his orders from you, and then he'll deal with Maynard."

"Is there a reason for this, my lord?" Gerald looked concerned.

"He needs seasoning, Gerald, and it'll be good practice for you."

"Commanding knights? Why would I need practice commanding knights?"

"Not knights specifically, but learning to deal with problems is an essential element of command."

"You don't want to deal with him yourself, do you?"

Fitz smiled, "There, you've mastered your first lesson. Now, I must be off; I have things to attend to."

He left his friend in the courtyard, a bewildered look on the younger man's face.

He found Sir Lionel guarding the prisoner. She had been moved, and now was held in a room attached to a long corridor, which ended in a chamber where the knight sat, oiling his weapon. "My lord," he said, rising to his feet as Lord Richard entered.

"How is the prisoner?" asked Fitz.

"Quiet," the knight responded.

"You won't be needed anymore, Sir Lionel. I have made other arrangements for her guard."

"My lord?"

"You are dismissed. Return to your regular duties, but remember, you are not to breathe a word of this prisoner to anyone, and the same applies to Sir Maynard. See to it that he understands."

"Yes, Lord," Sir Lionel replied, gathering up his sword.

Fitz waited while the man left, his footsteps echoing away into nothingness. He grabbed the torch from the wall, making his way down the hallway. There was a total of six rooms here, each with its own bed, desk and chair. They must, he reasoned, have been built to house more important prisoners, though he struggled to think of any time in the past when that had been necessary. The doors were wooden, each with a barred window displaying those within. As the only prisoner currently abiding within, the woman had the place to herself.

He knocked on the door and waited patiently. When there was no reply, he repeated his actions.

"I am your prisoner," the woman responded. "Why do you insist on playing this ridiculous charade? If you want to enter, just enter."

"I didn't want to intrude," said Fitz, opening the door. The woman was sitting on the edge of the bed, staring at the doorway. "I wish to apologize for your earlier treatment. My brother has assigned me as your jailer; I am to see that you are provided for. Is there anything you need?"

"My freedom," the prisoner requested.

"I'm afraid that isn't possible. I must do my duty."

"Duty? That's just a word to hide behind, to do unpleasant things."

Fitz was incensed, "Without duty, all would be chaos. Duty keeps the peace, allows people to live their lives safely."

"You're wrong," she responded, "life IS chaos, the survival of the fittest. The strong devour the weak."

"No, that's not true," retorted Fitz. "It's the obligation of the strong to look after the weak."

"You're a fool if you believe that," she replied.

"Am I? Then you must also be a fool. You called off the animals when they attacked us. Why?"

"To avoid their deaths," she answered.

"Exactly, to protect them. If you truly believed the strong devour the weak, then you should have left them to be slaughtered."

She sat in silence for a moment, before responding, "I will concede the point, but I still maintain my argument for most cases. Isn't it the motto of the army, that might makes right?"

"I can't argue with that," Fitz agreed, "but I have been raised with my obligation to protect others."

"Your father must have been a most unusual man," she said, "for I fear he did not hold ideas common to most."

"Not really," he countered. "My father had little to do with my upbringing, but he did instill in me my sense of duty. It used to be more common to follow the old ways of the nobility, but the fashion nowadays seems to be unbridled greed and power."

Both remained silent while Fitz tried to organize his thoughts.

"I wonder," the prisoner said finally, "if I might not have another blanket, it gets rather cold down here."

Fitz seized upon the morsel of conversation, "Of course, I will see to it immediately. I'll also see if I can find you some warmer clothes. Do you, perchance, read?"

"Yes," she responded, "why do you ask?"

"You're likely to be here for a while," he acknowledged. "Reading would allow you to pass the time. We have a number of books in the Keep; I'm told my mother was an avid reader. I can bring you some if you like?"

"Very well," she said, "I might as well put my time to use while I'm here."

"Then I will leave you, Madam, while I see to your requests." He left the room, careful to lock the door behind him. He still felt uneasy about her captivity but knew he dared not go against the wishes of his brother.

The warmer weather had come, and Lord Richard made his way to the prisoner. It had become a ritual, every morning and evening he would bring her food and ensure she had water to last the day. Today he had selected another book to bring her, for she had proved to be a voracious reader.

He knocked on her door, as was his custom, and then waited for her to say 'enter' before unlocking it. He laid the platter of food on her table and then grabbed the book he had tucked under his arm. "I noticed you had finished the last one I brought you, so I fetched you another," he said, handing her the tome.

She picked it up, opening the cover to examine the title page, "The Merchant and the Prince," she read out loud. "I've heard of this."

"Yes," Fitz proudly announced, "by the great writer, Califax."

"I'm quite familiar with his works," she announced.

Now it was Fitz's turn to be surprised, "You've read Califax?"

"That surprises you? I didn't always live in the woods, you know. I was born in Tewsbury."

"How did you come to live in the Whitewood?" he enquired.

"It's a long story," she answered.

"We have plenty of time," he suggested.

"Another day, perhaps," she replied, flipping through the pages. "I visited the great library in Shrewesdale years ago. There is a statue of Califax."

"I've never been," admitted Fitz, "though I imagine it as a great city. I know it used to be the cultural capital of Merceria."

"That was a long time ago," she reminded him. "It's an old city now, run down and corrupted by those in power, but the librarians were most helpful. I studied there for some years."

Fitz was taken aback, "You studied there? So you had an education, then?"

"No, I studied there myself. I knew how to read, but I was self-taught. What better place to learn than a library with the collected wisdom of the kingdom? I used to make copious notes."

"Perhaps," he offered, "you'd like to write? I can arrange ink and parchment if you wish."

"I think I should like that," she replied. "That's most kind of you."

It was several days later when Fitz observed Gerald leading a patrol of men back through the gate. With his own responsibilities keeping him occupied, he was pleased to see his friend carrying on in his absence.

He nodded as Gerald dismounted. "How goes it?" Fitz asked.

"Well, my lord," his protege replied.

Fitz had heard a slight hesitation in Gerald's voice, "Something wrong?"

"It's Sir Maynard, my lord."

"What of him?"

"He's been causing… problems," again the hesitation.

"Spit it out, man," Fitz commanded. "What type of problems?"

"He's been speaking ill of you, Lord," Gerald replied. "I told him to guard his tongue, but he told me to mind my own business."

"What did Sir Rodney do?" asked Fitz.

"He wasn't with us; he had to investigate another animal attack."

"Another? I thought they'd stopped."

"No, far from it. If anything, they've picked up in the last few weeks."

Fitz frowned, no doubt he would be asked to talk to the prisoner again. He must make an effort to find out more.

"Where is Sir Maynard now?"

"He mentioned something about the dungeons, though I might have misheard him."

Fitz immediately grew worried, a look that was not lost on his friend.

"Is something wrong, Lord?"

"No, Gerald. See to your horse; I have some unfinished business to attend to. I'll catch up with you later."

"Aye, Lord," the man replied.

Lord Richard rushed to the dungeons, worried for the prisoner's safety. Would Sir Maynard try to seek retribution by killing her? He arrived to find things as he had left them. A knock on the door resulted in the woman's usual response. He opened it to see her sitting at the table, her hand holding a quill hovering over a parchment.

"What are you writing?" he asked.

"Just some random thoughts," she replied. "Is it mealtime already?"

"No, I had some free time, so I thought I might visit." He moved closer to the table, and his eyes glanced over her notes. "I fancy myself an accomplished reader," he said, "but I can't make head nor tail of that."

"It's an ancient language," she said.

"Elvish?"

"No, older. It's amazing what you can learn from ancient texts, though I fear I haven't mastered it."

"Is there anything you have need of?" he asked.

"My freedom?" she responded. "Oh wait, let me guess, it's not within your power."

He nodded in agreement.

"Then nothing," she responded, "though I thank you for your visit, it's lonely here without my friends."

"Friends? Perhaps I can contact them for you, let them know where you are."

"I don't' think that would be wise; they're not Human."

"Orcs?"

"No, animals. I doubt you'd be able to communicate with them."

"You can speak to them, can't you?" he suddenly realized.

"Yes, though not in the traditional sense. I have to use magic."

"Did you command them to attack our hunters?"

"I can talk to them; I don't control them."

"You seemed to control them when we found you."

"That was different, I was asking them."

"Would the animals stop attacking us if you asked them to?" he persisted.

"And why would I do that? Have you stopped hunting them?"

"No," he reluctantly admitted, "we're running short of food."

"Then they do what they must to survive," she said, "though I fear many more may die before this affair is settled. Tell your men to stop hunting, and the attacks will halt."

"You know I can't do that. My brother would never agree."

"Then release me, and I'll see what I can do."

"You know I can't do that either. Tell me, if we did stop hunting, would that truly end the attacks?"

"I cannot say for certain," she replied, "but I think it would be likely."

"I will give it some thought," Fitz promised. "Perhaps I can find some way of convincing him."

"I have a sense that time is running out," she said, somewhat cryptically.

"What do you mean?" he asked.

"I cannot say for sure; I sometimes have flashes of insight. I fear something big is coming."

"I'll keep your thoughts in mind," he said, turning to leave. "Perhaps my brother will be in a more amenable mood tomorrow."

He stepped through the door, deep in thought and turned to lock it. A shape came seemingly from nowhere, and a blinding pain surged through his head. He staggered back only to see the form of Sir Maynard, towering over him, dropping a stick to the ground. Suddenly the knight's strong hands gripped him around the neck, choking the very life out of him. The room swirled, and he fought to maintain consciousness. He grasped the young man's strong arms in an effort to pull them from his throat, but the knight's fingers were locked securely around him. His eyes began to bulge, and he felt himself slipping on the floor.

Sir Maynard drove him back against the wall, holding him up with his youthful strength, Fitz's feet dangling as the knight tightened his grip. The room was going black. Sir Maynard's face was pressed close to his, and then the knight's eyes suddenly held a look of surprise. His grip slackened, leaving Fitz looking on in disbelief as thin vines began to erupt from the man's neck, growing thicker as he watched.

His throat released, he slipped to the floor, but the body of Sir Maynard seemed suspended in the air. The woman was standing in the doorway to the cell, her hands gesticulating in front of her. The floor had exploded beneath his enemy, and now another large, thick vine erupted from the floor to pierce Sir Maynard's back and protrude from his mouth. There were even flowers budding on the vine, adding to the macabre vision.

He stared for what seemed an eternity, his mind struggling to make sense of what he had witnessed. "Thank you," he stammered. "You saved my life."

She lowered her hands, "I regret having to kill the man," she said, "but I saw no other choice. It was either him or you. I'm afraid I've sealed my fate. The baron won't look kindly upon having one of his men killed. He'll want me executed."

"What did you do?" he asked.

"I used vines," she explained. "It's a spell."

"But they erupted from stone," he remarked.

"No, they erupted from the earth below the stone. I can't conjure from stone; I'm not that kind of Earth Mage."

He looked at her with new eyes, "With power like that, you could have escaped at any time. Why didn't you?"

"Would the hunting have stopped?" she asked.

"No, but at least you'd be free."

"You'd just send even more soldiers to hunt me down. At least by my being here, things are not escalating."

Fitz looked at the body of Sir Maynard, still shaking slightly from his ordeal. The body remained suspended in the air, impaled by the vines. "Can you reverse the spell?" he asked.

"You mean remove the vine? Certainly, but why?"

"I'm going to save your life," he answered. "Please, proceed with your spell."

She began the incantation, and he watched her hands swirling about in front of her, the effect almost mesmerizing. Moments later, he heard a sound like creaking wood and the vines began to recede, growing smaller until they disappeared into the floor. Only the bare earth beneath the displaced stones bore evidence that anything had happened, save for the body lying upon them.

Fitz drew his sword and started swinging at the body.

"What are you doing?" the woman yelled.

"Covering up the cause of death. Nobody will look closely; the man attacked me, and I defended myself. You won't take the blame."

"Why would you do that?" she asked. "Take the blame for my actions?"

"You saved my life," he responded, "and it's the right thing to do."

She looked on in silence as he completed his work.

"There," he said at last, "now I just have to haul his carcass out of here."

"You must lock me back up," she reminded him, "or someone might suspect I had a hand in this."

He nodded and fetched his keys. He was about to close the door when he paused. "I'm curious," he said, "why is the Whitewood so important to you?"

"It's my home," she replied, "and we must maintain the balance."

"The balance?"

"Yes, all things must be in balance or everyone suffers."

"I'm not sure I understand what you mean," he searched for clarification.

"If wolves hunt the deer to extinction their own survival is in jeopardy. The same is true of Humans. Imagine if you hunted all the animals from the woods, there would be nothing left. Without the animals, even the plants would begin to suffer. Nature is a delicately balanced environment, if one thing gets upset, the entire system suffers."

"So you're saying that if we over-hunt the Whitewood, there will be repercussions."

"Yes, though some might not be seen for many years."

"You're a wise woman," he proclaimed.

"You may call me Albreda," she offered, "for that's my name."

"Very well, Albreda. I thank you for saving my life. I shall do all I can to repay that kindness."

-Interlude II-

BODDEN

Summer 960 MC

B aron Richard Fitzwilliam sat back in his chair, taking a deep drink of his wine. "That was how she saved my life," he said, "though I never told anyone about it till now."

Anna scrunched up her face, "I'm confused. She saved your life and yet she felt compelled to come and help you? That doesn't make much sense."

"I'm betting," said Beverly, "that my father hasn't finished the tale. He's drawing it out. Isn't that right, Father?"

Fitz laughed, "You know me too well, my dear. There is indeed more to the story. But surely someone else has a tale to tell?"

"Oh no," said Anna, "you must keep telling us your tale now that you've started."

"Did you ever reconcile with your brother?" asked Hayley.

"I'm afraid not," said Fitz. "It wasn't long after this that Albreda's prophesy came true. Still, I'm getting a little ahead of myself; it was still some two months away from the coming siege."

"I remember Sir Maynard's death, though I can't say it surprised me," reflected Gerald. "At least now I know why you didn't lead any patrols. I thought you were training me."

"I was, my dear fellow, and you did a magnificent job. If it weren't for you, we would have been finished."

"I should have stopped Sir Maynard," Gerald commiserated.

"Don't be silly," said Fitz. "You had no way of knowing. No, it worked out for the best in the end."

There was a silence as he sat in contemplation.

"Well?" prompted Anna.

"Well what, Your Highness?" asked Fitz.

"Father," said Beverly, "we're waiting for the rest of the story."

"Oh yes, of course," the baron continued, "Now, where was I. Let's see, oh yes I'd just learned Albreda's name and promised to talk to my brother..."

Fitz and the Witch: Part III

THE MAGE IN THE TOWER

Spring 933 MC

T he view from the map room always impressed Lord Richard. The entire barony could be surveyed from here, and if it weren't for his brother always being in the room, he would spend more time up here overlooking the land. The door opened, and Edward entered as if summoned by Lord Richard's very thoughts.

"Brother," said the baron, "I'm surprised to see you here, you've been so quiet of late."

"I might have a solution to our problem," offered Fitz.

"Remind me again which problem we are referring to?"

"The animal attacks."

"Oh, that again? Very well, what do you propose?"

Lord Richard gathered his thoughts, "If we stop hunting in the Whitewood, the animal attacks will end."

"Again, Brother? I'm tired of hearing this."

"It's true; the animals are only attacking to protect their land."

"Don't be daft, animals attack because they're animals. With their leader in chains, there's no one to command them. Sooner or later we'll have them all hunted down, and then the attacks will be over."

"And how many people must die before then?" demanded Fitz angrily.

"As many as it takes," replied the baron. "They're doing what needs to be done. Certainly, sacrifices will have to be made for the greater good, but we will win through in the end."

"How can you be so callous about the loss of life?" exclaimed Lord Richard.

Edward turned on him quickly, "I am the baron, and it is my decision who lives and dies. The running of the barony is my responsibility, Brother. You may not agree with my decisions, but they carry the weight of law." Fitz watched his brother once again stopping himself, taking a deep breath and letting it out slowly in an attempt to calm himself.

"I know you mean well," the baron continued, "but you cannot trust the word of a witch. In time you'll see for yourself. Perhaps it would be best if I had her executed. If we hang her from the walls, maybe the enemy would back down."

"I forbid it," declared Fitz.

"You forget who you're talking to, Richard. I am the baron here."

"Yes," he agreed, "and you gave me responsibility for the prisoner, that includes the choice over life and death."

"Very well," said the baron in resignation, "have it your way. We won't execute her, but the prisoner remains here, at the Keep."

The door opened, and Albreda looked up to see Lord Richard Fitzwilliam standing in the doorway. "I've decided to move you," he said, without preamble.

"Move me? To where?" she asked.

"There are four small towers at the top of the Keep; I'm moving you to one of them. You'll still be a prisoner, but you'll have fresh air and daylight. I must ask you to promise not to attempt to escape."

"Why would you trust my word? I could simply agree, and then escape anyway."

"While that's true, I believe you to be an honourable woman. I will take you at your word until I have a reason not to."

"Very well, I give you my word. When will I be moved?"

"Late this evening. You can't be seen; my brother still wishes to keep your presence here a secret."

"Is he afraid that the animals might attack the Keep? I can honestly say that's quite unlikely."

"No, but he fears your magic. I don't want to bring any more attention to you than already exists."

"Won't my presence be noticed by the guards?"

"No, the towers are mostly ornamental, and the guards don't use them. Sir Rodney will have command of the watch; he'll make sure no one goes near the tower you'll be housed in. I know it's not the best arrangement, but at least you won't be locked down here."

"I thank you for this small kindness."

It didn't take long to move her. Lord Richard had arranged to have furniture waiting, and so he merely escorted her to the tower in the middle of the night. Sir Rodney kept the watch busy on the other side of the Keep, and she was soon ensconced in her new accommodations. It was a small room, only several paces across, with a single window that looked to the east and heavy shutters to close should the weather require it.

Albreda settled in without complaint, and Fitz left her to get some sleep, returning at first light. He was carrying a new book for her and knocked quietly, in case she was still resting from the late night activities. He opened the door to see her standing by the window, silhouetted against the rising sun. She turned as he entered, a smile on her face for the first time since he had met her.

"Lord Richard," she said, "I trust nothing is amiss?"

"There's been another attack," he informed her.

"I know," she replied. "I'm afraid they may continue until we can come to an agreement."

"You control the animals," he persisted. "Please tell them to stop."

"As I've explained to you before; I don't control them. They make their own decisions."

"But you can advise them," he reminded her.

"I see no reason to," she stated.

"I understand your reluctance," he continued, "but we need to hunt. The farms aren't producing enough food, and with the Norland raids over the winter, we're stretched to the limit."

"There are other places to hunt," she suggested.

He was ready to counter her argument, but her logic surprised him. "What do you mean?" he pressed.

"Only the Whitewood is my concern," she explained. "Let the men of Bodden hunt elsewhere."

"Where?" he asked. "We don't have the time or manpower to search for richer grounds."

"What if I found a better place for you to hunt? Would the baron stop hunting my friends?"

"Surely," he responded. "But how would you do that from here?"

"You might be surprised at what I can do," she said, "but you must trust me. I will need to cast a spell."

His trepidation must have been evident, for she quickly added, "I swear my spell will do no harm, nor allow me to escape."

"Very well," he reluctantly agreed, "you may cast your spell."

"Thank you," she said. "I will begin casting in just a moment; it's important that you don't interrupt my concentration while I'm undertaking the spell."

"How will I know when you're done?" he asked.

"You'll see my hands stop moving. Now, are you ready?"

"As ready as I'm ever going to be," he stated.

She gazed out of the window and starting chanting, the words barely audible to Lord Richard. He couldn't make out anything he recognized, but it felt as if the air suddenly went calm. She kept muttering, and then stretched her arms out the window, holding them there until a bird quite unexpectedly landed on them. She brought her limbs back inside, and Fitz was amazed to see a wild falcon perched on her arm. She bowed her forehead, and the bird placed its head against it. There was a moment of shared space, and then the bird leaped from its perch, flying out the window.

Fitz watched the entire scene play out before him, afraid of disturbing it. "What just happened?" he asked at last.

"I have sent him to search the area for game. He'll come back when he finds it in sufficient numbers."

"How long is that likely to take?" he asked.

"A couple of days, perhaps?" she guessed. "It depends on what he finds."

The great hall at Bodden Keep was busy with activity. Lord Edward Fitzwilliam, Baron of Bodden, sat in his usual chair while all around him food was being served. The complete complement of knights was present, for he had ordered a feast to be prepared. He was in a particularly good mood this day, though his cheerfulness seemed to dull as his brother, Lord Richard Fitzwilliam, entered the room.

"How goes it, Brother?" asked Lord Richard, in a particularly jovial tone.

"It goes well," answered the baron, suspicion creeping into his voice. "Why do you ask?"

"No particular reason. It's an especially warm day today, don't you think?"

"I suppose so," muttered the baron, returning to his food.

"Sir Rodney," said Lord Richard, ignoring his brother's disdain, "how goes the hunt?

"It is going particularly well, Lord," the knight responded. "The new area is proving most bountiful."

"New area?" said Lord Edward, looking up from his plate abruptly. "What new area?"

Sir Rodney, who was about to drink his wine, carefully placed his flagon back on the table. "To the southwest, Lord. 'Twas your brother who suggested it."

Edward looked upset, and Fitz wondered if he was about to unleash a tirade against him. It was unlikely to happen with the knights present, but he had seen his brother do stranger things on occasion.

The baron beckoned him to his side to whisper, "What are you up to, Brother. I told you not to mess with things."

"No," Richard replied, "you wanted a solution; I have given you one. Tell me Sir Rodney," he continued, raising his voice, "how many animal attacks have we suffered in the last few weeks?"

"None," reported the knight. "Everything is calm."

They spoke no more of it until the knights had had their fill. Now, the two brothers sat, drinking their wine, as the servants cleaned up the mess.

"It's safe now," said Fitz, "you can release her. There's no reason to keep her prisoner any longer."

"You're wrong, Brother," the baron replied. "We need to keep her as a hostage against future attacks. As long as I'm the baron, she'll remain in Bodden Keep."

-Interlude III-

BODDEN

Summer 960 MC

"That explains how the attacks stopped," said Hayley.

"Yes," said Beverly, growing more exasperated, "but it still doesn't explain Albreda's promise. Why did she come to our aid during the siege?"

Fitz smiled, "I was true to my word, while my brother was baron, she remained a prisoner."

"Wait," said Gerald, "I remember now. When Sir James told you that you were the new baron, you said you had something to take care of."

"That's right, my friend, I had to release Albreda."

"Oh no," said Anna, "you're not getting out of it that easily. I want details; your story's not over yet."

"Very well, Your Highness," the baron said, "I shall tell you the rest. It was right after the siege."

"Wait a moment," said Hayley, "what siege. We were at the siege; I don't remember a prisoner."

"Not that siege, that was more recent," explained Beverly.

"How many sieges have there been, exactly," asked Hayley.

It was Gerald who answered her question, "Three in recent memory. The first took place back when I was young."

"That's where you killed your first Norlander," provided Anna.

"Yes, that's right," the baron interjected. "The second siege was when my brother was killed."

"That must be the one in your story, where Albreda was a prisoner," said Anna, a triumphant look on her face.

"Yes, Your Highness. Gerald and I led a small band to take out the enemy catapults. While we were returning, an explosion lit up the wall that was under construction. The devastation was terrible…"

Fitz and the Witch: Part IV

THE PROMISE

Summer 933 MC

F itz stood amongst the rubble of the wall, staring in disbelief.

"You are the baron now, Lord," stated Sir James. "What is your will?"

Fitz looked about him at the destruction. He had never wanted this. Even though he had always argued with his brother since he became the baron, they were still family. Edward's death hit him hard, but he knew he must take action, for he was now responsible for the defence of Bodden.

"Place guards on this wall. I doubt the Norlanders will attack again. We've broken their will." He turned to his stalwart companion, "Gerald, see that this wall is shored up as best you can. Sir James?"

"My lord?" replied the knight.

"You will take orders from Sergeant Matheson here. Do as he says." He was about to leave when the knight objected.

"He's not a noble, my lord."

Fitz turned to berate the man, but his energy was sapped; it was all too much to take in. "He has my complete confidence to carry out my will," he spat out, perhaps with more venom that he wished, "and I am the new baron, correct?"

"Of course, my lord," replied Sir James.

"Then do as I say. Gerald, when you've got this secured, meet me in the map room. I have something else to attend to first." He wondered if Albreda was still safe, for the catapults had been merciless in their assault, and he had had not yet had time to check on her.

"Aye, Lord," replied Gerald, and began barking out orders.

He made his way to Albreda's room, knocking on the door as he always did. As her voice beckoned, he opened it to enter. She was standing at the window and turned as he came in.

"I trust all is well?" she asked.

"My brother is dead," he declared, "and while it grieves me to think of it, it means I'm the baron now."

"I'm sorry for your loss," she said with sympathy in her voice.

"Really?" he responded fiercely. "I should think you would be elated at the death of your captor."

"Death is never to be celebrated," she explained, an easy confidence to her voice. "It is not something I would wish on anyone, despite our differences. Your brother acted according to his conscience, I cannot fault him for that. What will happen now?"

"I'm releasing you," said Fitz. "You're free to go."

"You're releasing me? After all this time?"

"Yes," he affirmed. "You should have been released long ago, but it wasn't within my power. Now that I'm the baron, it's my decision."

"Just like that? I can walk out of here?" she asked in disbelief.

"Yes, just like that. I'll escort you to the gate myself; my troops are a little busy cleaning up from the siege. I trust you weren't injured?"

"No," she answered. "The catapults came nowhere near me, but you look like you've seen some fighting."

Fitz looked down at his armour, still covered with dirt and blood, "I suppose I have. If you'd like to gather your things, I'll lead you out."

"Thank you," she said. "I've little to gather, other than my notes. I do wish to thank you for the clothes you have provided; I will leave them here."

"You may keep them," he offered, "they are no use to me."

She smiled and bowed her head slightly, "I thank you, Lord, or should I say, Baron. Please, lead on."

He guided her down through the Keep. In the wake of the siege, the people were far too busy to take note of the two of them as they descended the stairwell.

"I want to thank you for the treatment you've bestowed on me during my captivity. You've been most gracious."

"I'm only sorry," said Fitz, "that things couldn't have been resolved sooner."

"What will happen after I'm gone?" she asked.

"I will give orders that none of my men will hunt in the Whitewood, that shall be your domain. I will leave instructions that the woods are to be left undisturbed and ensure that the agreement is passed down to future generations."

"I thank you for that. In exchange, I will promise to keep control of the animals that live therein; your people will be safe."

They had reached ground level and were crossing the courtyard when Albreda stopped suddenly, using a hand to steady herself against a wall. Fitz, looking at her intensely, noticed that her eyes were closed; she was breathing heavily as if she had just completed a great exertion.

"Are you all right-"

She raised her hand to forestall his enquiry. He could see her struggling with some sort of inner turmoil, and then she opened her eyes, exhaling as she did so. "Everything is fine," she said quietly. "I've just had a vision, it happens sometimes."

"A vision?"

"Yes, I saw a shadow approaching. A siege is coming," she said.

Fitz was confused, "We just broke a siege."

"True, but it won't be the last. At some point in the future, when shadows are falling over the kingdom, Bodden will be the rock that breaks the waves. You must hold firm, Baron Richard, and I will come to return the favour you have bestowed on me this day."

The two walked on in silence until they reached the outer gate, "May I offer you a horse, Mistress Albreda?"

The woman smiled, "Just call me Albreda, I've never been keen on the term mistress."

"Very well, Albreda," he said, returning the smile. "Still, the offer stands. A horse?"

"No, thank you. I think I prefer to walk. Long life to you Baron, until our paths cross again."

He watched her as she walked across the now abandoned siege lines, wondering about the strange portent she had shared. She picked her way carefully through the ruined camp and the last he saw of her, there were three wolves running toward her. He knew she was home.

-Interlude IV-

BODDEN

Summer 960 MC

T he room was silent after the baron finished his story.

"It all makes so much sense now," said Beverly. "Why is it you've never told me this story before, Father?"

"Well," Fitz ruminated, "it happened before you were born. I married your mother shortly thereafter, and then you came along. It didn't seem to have any relevance."

"It does now," observed Princess Anna.

"I'm glad you think so, Your Highness, but at the time, it meant nothing."

"Did you see her again over the years?" asked Hayley.

"No, I didn't see again until you broke the siege."

"But," offered Anna, "there must have been some connection between you two."

"I only had eyes for Lady Evelyn," Fitz responded. "I respected Albreda, but I wasn't in love with her."

"The princess has a romantic side," explained Gerald. "She only wishes for a happy ending."

"Don't we all," said Hayley. "Still, life's not really like that. We don't just magically find our soul mate. Isn't that right, Beverly?"

Beverly was staring off into the distance, so the ranger tapped her on the arm, "Beverly?"

"Sorry," Beverly apologized. "I was just lost in thought there. What were you saying?"

"I was saying," Hayley repeated, "that there's no such thing as a soul mate."

Beverly smiled, "I don't believe that's true. I'd like to think that some people find their ideal companion. It gives a person hope."

"You said earlier," interrupted Anna, "that Albreda saw the library in Shrewesdale. I'd love to visit it someday."

"I've been there," offered Beverly, "and it's quite impressive, though I didn't spend much time in it."

"You were in Shrewesdale?" the princess asked.

"Yes, I spent some time there, though it didn't end well."

"Why," Anna asked, "what happened?"

"I'd rather not talk about it. It brings back unpleasant memories. It wasn't all bad, though. While I was in service to the countess all sorts of things happened, some of them were quite amusing."

"I sense it's time for another tale," said Gerald. "It seems the Fitzwilliams are the master storytellers this evening."

Anna beamed, "Please Beverly, tell us about of one of your adventures in Shrewesdale. You can leave out the bad parts if you prefer."

Beverly smiled, "Very well, Your Highness, I'll tell you the story of the Bandit King."

"That sounds exciting," said Anna, settling back against her faithful companion.

"It all started back in the summer of '55. I had arrived in the city the previous spring, to begin my service to the Countess of Shrewesdale…"

Beverly and the Bandit King: Part I

Summer 955 MC

T here was a cool breeze blowing down the street, evaporating the sweat from Beverly as she sat outside the Crow's Foot Tavern. Across from her, Olivia scanned the street, watching as the townsfolk went about their business. Beverly took a swig of her wine, immediately feeling the coolness in her throat. This was one of the warmer days of summer, and she found herself missing the cooler climate of Bodden.

"Looks like something's up," mused Olivia, looking down the street. Beverly followed her friend's gaze to the eastern gate, where a group of horsemen rode through.

"What do you make of it?" asked Beverly.

"Looks like knights," the older woman replied, "though I daresay they don't look happy."

Covered in dust and dirt, they removed their helmets to reveal scowls on their faces.

"Something's gone amiss, I suspect," said Olivia. "I bet they've been having problems with the Bandit King again."

"Bandit King? I don't think I've heard of him."

"Really? I'd have thought you'd know all about him," Olivia responded, then, seeing Beverly's look of bewilderment, she decided to elucidate. "He leads a group of bandits that have been robbing merchants in the Shrewes-dale Hills. They say he disappears quickly, and he's proving to be difficult to find."

"Isn't Bandit King a rather grandiose title for a thief?"

"Oh, word is he came up with that himself. The earl's had it out for him ever since he intercepted a shipment of the lord's favourite wine. Stole it off the wagon and sent the driver back with an empty load."

"I imagine the earl must have been furious," observed Beverly.

"He was. He executed the driver for allowing it to happen."

Beverly was shocked, "Executed him? Why would he do that, it's not as if it was the driver's fault."

"That's our earl," offered Olivia. "He's a man who's quick to anger, and it is said he never forgets a slight."

Beverly shuddered. She tried to imagine her father in a similar situation, but couldn't conceive of him doling out such a harsh punishment. He believed in fairness and justice, apparently traits which the earl did not share.

The riders made their way up the street, and as they passed the Crow's Foot, one of their number halted, dismounting to tie his horse to a post. There was no mistaking the man, for his six-foot frame instantly gave him away.

"Sir Heward," called out Beverly, "how goes the patrol?"

The massive knight, turning at the sound of his name, frowned slightly as he recognized her. "Dame Beverly," he replied, somewhat formally.

His speech was stilted, and he was obviously uncomfortable around her, but it was understandable. Beverly had defeated him in single combat shortly after her arrival in Shrewesdale, and yet the man had not born a grudge, treating her with nothing but respect since. She watched him wander inside, heading straight toward the bar, and then she rose from her seat to follow. "I'll be back in a moment, Olivia. I'm going to see what else I can dig up."

Olivia watched her friend disappear and smiled. She knew Beverly would never let this rest. It would be interesting to see what she could discover.

Sir Heward was just raising his ale to his lips when Beverly appeared beside him. He ignored her presence, taking a deep gulp, then set the drink down on the countertop. He reluctantly turned to face her, as if dealing with a small child. "Well?" he said expectantly.

Beverly smiled, "Sir Heward, tell me, how goes the hunt for the Bandit King."

Heward turned back, avoiding her question to take another deep drink.

"That bad, is it?" she probed.

He took yet another swig but remained facing the bar when he answered her, "The bastard's impossible to find. By the time we even hear of an attack, he's long gone. Riding around the hills isn't helping; he can probably hear us from miles away. All we're doing is tiring the horses and sweating like pigs in this heat."

"Sounds like a job for a King's Ranger," mused Beverly.

Heward laughed before responding, "A King's Ranger? Aye, that would be grand, but the earl won't admit he needs help, so he keeps sending us out to search for the beggar. We've been out six times this week alone. We rode out twice yesterday, all because of rumours. I tell you, the man's a ghost."

"How many people has he killed?" Beverly asked.

"Killed? I don't think the man's actually killed anyone. He and his band of thieves typically rob merchants and then send them on their way. He's attacked six in the last fortnight alone."

"How does he know when a trader is approaching?" she asked.

"Beats me, but it wouldn't be too hard to set up some of his men to watch the road. As you're no doubt aware, the country around here is very uneven, not exactly prime terrain for knights."

"Maybe I should look into it," she mused.

"You?" Heward turned to laugh at her. "No offence, Dame Beverly, but what makes you think you can do anything when all the earl's men have failed?"

Beverly smiled, "Simple, I'm a woman."

She dropped a coin onto the bar. "Another drink for my friend here, barkeep," she offered.

Heward raised his cup in salute, "Good luck to you then, Dame Beverly, I suspect you'll need it."

Lady Catherine Montrose, Countess of Shrewesdale, was wife to the Earl of Shrewesdale. As the daughter of the previous earl, her younger husband had inherited the title when he married her, though Beverly suspected it was more to do with her wealth than her title.

Now she sat in her favourite reading room as Beverly entered, bowing before her mistress.

"Beverly," the old woman said, "I trust you have been keeping yourself busy?"

"Yes, Your Grace," she replied.

"You have served me faithfully for the last year, and I must admit I have been quite pleased with your accomplishments. You have removed the stain upon my house and stopped the knights from their lecherous behaviour toward my servants, and for that, I am truly thankful."

A worried look crossed Beverly's mind. Was she about to be dismissed from her service?

The countess held up her hand as if she could read minds, "Fear not, Beverly, I am not getting rid of you. After much deliberation on my part, I have decided to ask you to perform a task for me."

"Of course, Your Grace," responded Beverly. "Whatever you need."

"Don't be so quick to respond, my young friend," the countess replied, "for I fear it might prove to be beyond even your capabilities."

"You intrigue me, my lady. Please, tell me more."

"No doubt by now you've heard of the self-styled Bandit King?"

"Yes," said Beverly, "he's been raiding merchants on the Shrewesdale road. I hear he's been quite a nuisance."

"Quite so. The man needs to be brought to justice before someone is killed. My husband's knights have proven to be unequal to the task so far. I thought that perhaps you might like to have a crack at it."

"Me, Your Grace? What makes you think I could stop this Bandit King?"

"I have gotten know you, Dame Beverly. You think things through instead of charging in haphazardly. It will require cunning to bring this man to justice, and I think you're just the person for the job."

"I'm flattered, my lady, and in truth, I have already given it some thought."

"Excellent," said the countess. "I will authorize a purse for your expenses. It will likely take some time; I don't want you to rush it. I would rather wait and be successful, than have you hurry and fail. Come up with a plan and then report back to me. If I think it reasonable, you can proceed."

"Aye, my lady," Beverly solemnly swore, "I shall give it my best effort."

"As I knew you would," responded the countess.

It was late evening, a few days later, when Beverly sat at the Crow's Foot with Olivia, eating her meal absently as the two went over her plan.

"Are you sure about this?" asked Olivia.

"It's the only way," said Beverly. "I can't just ride down the road. At best, they'd just ignore me, and at worst they'd swarm me."

"Still, there has to be a better way."

"Listen," said Beverly, "the bandits attack merchants. If I look like a merchant, they're more likely to take the bait. Besides, I'll be a helpless woman; they won't be afraid of me."

"Shouldn't you at least wear your armour?"

Beverly looked at her friend for a moment in disbelief, "If you were a bandit, would you attack a wagon driven by a person in armour?"

"Hmmm, probably not. I suppose that makes sense. Still, I don't like it, it sounds dangerous."

"Oh, it will be if they get close enough," swore Beverly.

"What are you going to do about weapons? Won't a sword be somewhat obvious?"

"I'm going to carry a concealed dagger."

"That's it? A dagger? Are you out of your mind?" Olivia's voice increased with each question.

"I'm quite comfortable with all weapons. I can't really conceal anything bigger, and I'll simply take one of their swords if I get into trouble."

"Well, you're certainly confident."

"They're bandits, not trained soldiers. More than likely just a bunch of youths picking on easy targets. So far they've only attacked lone wagons without guards. I don't think there'll be much of a fight."

Olivia pondered the statement before answering, "I hope you're right. I'd hate to think what you might be walking into otherwise."

"Now, how did you make out with my list?" asked Beverly, ignoring the comment.

Olivia looked down at the paper in front of her, "Thanks to the coin Her Grace provided, I've managed to get you a horse and wagon. You'll be carrying a mixture of goods including cloth, nails, food and so on. A pretty typical assortment for a small trader. I called in some favours, so I've been assured the cargo will look legitimate."

"Excellent!"

"It only remains for you to decide when to begin this madcap scheme of yours."

Beverly looked out the window, "I suppose it's too late to start today. I'll head out at first light, that way I'll be on the road they have been attacking by midday."

"Good idea," agreed Olivia. "According to Sir Heward, the bandits strike during the day. Traffic has been light lately, so you'll make a tempting target. Are you sure you don't want me to go with you?"

"I appreciate the offer," said Beverly earnestly, "but your brother needs you, and this'll be dangerous. With any luck, I'll be back in a couple of days."

"A couple of days? I thought you were just going to fight them when you found them?"

"There's no guarantee I'll meet them right away, and even if I do, I'll want to find their camp."

Olivia placed her hand over her friend's. "Be careful Beverly," she warned, "these are dangerous times, and they might be desperate."

"I'll be fine, Olivia," she promised, "and trust me, I can be dangerous when I need to be."

The sun was high as Beverly made her way along the winding road that twisted its way through the Shrewesdale Hills. She had expected to encounter the bandits long before now, but she was beginning to think she was on a fool's errand. Did she really think they would fall for her ruse? It was imperative that she keep alert, but the rhythmic bouncing of the wagon combined with the constant drone of the horse's hooves on the ground dulled her senses.

Just as her eyelids started to droop, her horse balked when a man stepped onto the road in front of her. The stranger indicated for her to stop, so she pulled back on the reins to slow the horse down.

"Who are you?" she yelled out, trying to sound scared.

"Don't move, and no harm will come to you," the man ordered.

She tried to memorize the outlaw's face, but he was unremarkable looking. His clothes were common to a peasant, and there was a rather crude looking knife tucked into his belt. Beverly quickly concluded that this man was not the one in charge.

As soon as she stopped the wagon, others appeared, rising out of the hills to either side of the road. It didn't take long for them to surround her wagon, and she soon spotted the man in charge, for his clothes gave him away. He was of average height, with a neatly trimmed black beard. The leather armour he wore was common to archers in the Mercerian army. The bow on the man's back looked to be in good shape. These clues gave credence to her conclusion that he was a military man at some point in his past. The other men in the group were attired like the man who had stopped her. If these were, in truth, bandits, they must have had rather slim pickings, she thought.

The leader came up to the wagon beside her. He was holding a sword in his hand, though not in a threatening manner. He held it comfortably as if used to its weight. This man, she thought, knows how to use it when necessary.

"Well," he said, "what do we have here? A young woman all alone on the road? We can't have that now, can we?"

As he spoke she felt the wagon jostle; men climbed up behind her, no doubt to examine their haul. She thought to strike out at the leader, but she knew she needed to find their base if she was to stop them once and for all.

"Tell me," the leader said, interrupting her thoughts, "what's your name, lass?"

He was smiling at her, and she wondered if he thought to charm her. She decided to play along, though she had little idea how to flirt. She thought of Olivia and tried to emulate her. "My name's Evelyn," she said, using her mother's name. It was always best to pick a name one could remember. She smiled in an effort to flirt, but it came out more like a grimace.

The Bandit King stared at her a moment, perhaps unsure of her intent. Beverly started to feel frustrated; if she couldn't convince him to take her back to his camp, this was all for naught. What would Olivia do, she thought again. She was afraid the man was about to send her on her way, so she reached down to the hem of her dress and pulled it up absently to scratch her leg. Perhaps a display of her bare flesh might keep him occupied? She had seen her friend do this to considerable effect back at the Crow's Foot.

Sure enough, the bandit leader smiled at her. "It would be criminal of us to allow you to travel un-escorted," he said. "I must insist that you come with us, to keep you safe."

There was unexpected grumbling from the men on the wagon. One of the older ones spoke up, "That was never part of the deal, Grumman," he said. "We don't take prisoners, we let them go."

"Shut up, old man," the leader ordered. "I'm the one in charge around here. If the lady wants to be safe, it's up to her."

He looked up at Beverly, and she knew that, despite her inexperience, she had somehow interested him. She felt uncomfortable, for she was entering unknown territory here, and aside from Olivia's stories, she had little experience in the ways of men. She responded, trying to sound nervous, "I would be most pleased," she said, "if you would protect me, sir. You look to be a most pleasant man." She mentally kicked herself. Surely the leader would see right through her ruse, but he simply smiled.

"There, you see lads? The lady wants my protection. Far be it from me to refuse her." He offered her his hand, and she climbed down to the ground.

"What are you going to do with my wagon?" she asked.

"We'll take it back with us to the camp," the leader replied, "but it'll take some time. We're going to cut over the hills; they'll join up with us later."

-Interlude V-

BODDEN

Summer 960 MC

"Weren't you afraid?" asked Anna. "The Bandit King might have attacked you.""The thought did cross my mind," explained Beverly, "but I was confident I could take him in a fight, even with just a dagger. As it turned out, however, half the men came with us; the rest took the wagon."

"That was very brave of you, my dear," said Fitz. "Interesting how you used your mother's name."

"Well, I could hardly use my real name. A red-haired woman named Beverly would have brought instant recognition, especially after the duel I fought."

"Duel?" asked Anna. "What duel?"

"Shortly after I arrived in Shrewesdale," clarified Beverly, "I was challenged to a duel by one of the knights."

"I bet that didn't end well for him," offered Gerald. "I've seen you fight."

"You trained me well, so the fight didn't last long. Sir Heward stopped it after I'd defeated a number of them."

"Sir Heward?" asked Hayley. "The same Sir Heward that helped us at Eastwood?"

"The same," she replied. "He also helped me when I left Shrewesdale. He is an honourable man."

"The man is also immensely large," said Gerald, "and he carries that big axe."

Beverly smiled, "Yes, the other knights call him 'The Axe' and trust me when I say he knows how to use it."

"Fascinating," said Anna, "but you're keeping us in suspense. You've already told us how you found the Bandit King, but you have yet to tell us how it ends. Obviously, there's more."

"Yes, of course, Your Highness. They ended up taking me to their camp."

"Where was this camp?" asked Hayley. "It must have been some distance from the road for the knights to be unable to find it."

Beverly made a face, "With a few exceptions, the Knights of Shrewesdale were useless. All those fools knew how to do was to bully their way about."

The anger in her voice caught the baron's attention. He had heard rumours concerning his daughter's disgrace in Shrewesdale, but he didn't want her to feel uncomfortable here, among her friends. "Pray, continue the story, my dear," he interrupted, "or I fear we shall still be discussing things into the wee hours of the morning."

A look of gratitude passed between Beverly and her father, and then she continued. "Hayley is right, the camp was quite some distance away from the road, and it took us till late afternoon to arrive..."

Beverly and the Bandit King: Part II

THE CAMP OF THE BANDIT KING

Summer 955 MC

The camp was little more than a clearing in the woods. There were some lean-tos arranged to one side, away from the three fire pits that had been set up. She could tell the group lacked experience in such matters, for if rain came, it would drain right into their makeshift shelters.

Save for the leader himself, the other bandits looked bedraggled. Their clothes were threadbare, and their weapons looked makeshift, likely cobbled together from old farm implements. Some even used crude clubs and staves, little more than tree branches. Was this truly the fearsome Bandit King, she wondered.

"Randall," the leader called out, and a middle-aged man, missing his front teeth, appeared at his side.

"Yes, boss?"

"Put this woman to work," he commanded. "Have her do the cooking, it's about time we had a decent meal."

"Aye, sir," the man replied. "Come with me lass, and I'll show you the way."

The bandit led her gently towards a large pot that was suspended over a fire, tended by a young lad. "This 'ere's the cooking pot, I'm afraid it's not much," he apologized. "Young Sam here'll help you out. He'll show you where the food is."

Beverly stared at the pot; this was quite unexpected. "You want me to cook for you?"

"Of course, what else would a woman do?" he questioned.

She stared at him and, realizing the implication, he blushed. "We're not going to harm you," he said. "I promise you. We don't hurt women, many of us had wives and daughters."

"Had?" Beverly questioned. "What do you mean, had?"

"Died mostly, that's why we're here now. We've nothing else to live for."

"So you rob people?"

"We're just surviving here, miss; we do what we have to."

"Evelyn," said Beverly, trying to endear herself to the man. "Please call me, Evelyn."

"Very well, Evelyn. I'll leave you with Sam here to get the meal going."

Randall left her alone with the young lad, and Beverly realized the depth of her predicament. She had gone out on patrols, fought the enemy, even ridden and camped with men, but never, in all her life, had she been required to cook. Where would she begin? She thought back to those patrols in Bodden; it seemed like ages ago. Gerald would typically get the pot boiling then drop in the food. How difficult could it be? She turned to the youngster at the fire, "Get some water, Sam, and we'll start boiling it. What do we have to work with?"

"Not much," responded the young lad, "mostly vegetables."

"All right," she said, "vegetable soup it is, then."

While the water started to boil, Sam brought out the food. Beverly dropped a carrot into the water, and the young lad looked at her strangely.

"Aren't you going to cut it up?" he asked.

"Pardon?" she said.

"The carrot. Aren't you going to cut it up?"

"Oh yes, of course, I just thought I'd do that after it's cooked."

"How do you expect to do that?" he asked. "The water will be boiling."

She looked at him, and a moment of fear crossed her face. "Good point," she conceded. "I guess I'm not very good at this."

"Here," said Sam, "let me help."

Beverly watched as the young man started chopping up the vegetables. "What do you do here," she asked, "apart from cutting up the food, that is?"

"I help out around the camp," he responded. "There's all sorts of things to do."

"How did you end up being a bandit?" she asked.

"That's a long story," he answered.

"We seem to have lots of time," she observed. "It's going to take all day to cook that soup."

The boy made a face, "All day? Are you crazy? What makes you think it's going to take all day?"

Beverly was completely out of her element, so she decided to change the subject. "We have lots of time, regardless, tell me your story. How long have you been living like this?"

"We came here when we lost our farm. Mother got sick, and my father couldn't do all the work. The crops didn't grow very well last year, and then the harvest came up short."

"What do you mean, came up short?"

"We didn't produce enough food. The earl took everything."

"Everything? He didn't leave you your share?"

"He demanded his yield. He said the farm owed him more bushels of wheat than we had. There was nothing left to eat. Then he took the farm away from us, said he couldn't afford to have us work there anymore."

Beverly was shocked. Her father taught her it was the lord's duty to look after his people; the Earl of Shrewesdale clearly had no such thoughts.

"That's when we were forced into the wilderness. Mother died over the winter," Sam said bitterly, "and we would have starved if the Bandit King hadn't arrived to save us."

"Who is this Bandit King?" she asked.

"Don't know," replied Sam, "but he came from the North. I think he's from some place named Wickfield; I heard him mention it once. Is that in Merceria?"

"Yes, it's near the northern border. He's a long way from home."

"Are you from the north?"

"Yes, though that was many years ago," she lied.

She looked around as the soup bubbled away. The camp was clearly ill-organized, and yet she saw signs that indicated some military touches, confirming her suspicions that this self-styled Bandit King was a soldier at some point, most likely a deserter.

Randall came over to the fire to check on their progress. Sam was dropping some herbs into the pot as he approached. "Smells good," he said. "When do you think it'll be ready?"

"Hours, yet," answered Beverly.

"Soon," added Sam at the same time.

Randall looked at Beverly with a look of confusion. Her story was beginning to unravel, and she knew she must distract the man. "Those lean-tos," she said, "you know they're going to get you wet."

"What?" he said. "How?"

"If it rains," she offered, "the water will drain downhill, right into your cover."

Randall stared off into the camp; the thought had obviously never entered his mind. "Well, where should we put them then?"

Beverly pointed north, "There, on the slight rise. The water will drain away from you."

Randall nodded his head in agreement, "You're a smart one. Anything else we should know?"

"Yes," she added, "your men should stop defecating all over the place. Dig a pit and do it there."

"Defecating?"

"Yes," she said. The man was clearly not understanding her. "Shitting," she clarified. She mentally cursed herself; these were simple folk, not used to the educated words of a lady of the nobility.

"Oh, aye, I understand."

"You're lucky a King's Ranger hasn't hunted you down, you know. The stench would give you all away."

The man blushed, "Sorry Mistress Evelyn, it's been such a long time since we've had a visitor in camp."

"Tell me," continued Beverly, "are all of you farmers?"

"Aye, 'cept for the King there," Randall explained. "We've all been kicked out of our farms by the earl's men. Most've lost family." He fell into silence.

"I'm sorry," she said, simply.

"Do you really think they'll send a King's Ranger?" he asked, fear creeping into his voice.

"I'm surprised it has happened already," she replied. "Perhaps you should consider giving yourselves up?"

"It's too late for that," Randall said, "the earl's already ordered our deaths, I'm afraid we have no choice."

She remembered Olivia's words, 'desperate men will do desperate things.' She pitied their position. Life had been hard on them, though it was her duty to bring them to justice. She balked at the thought; surely these men deserved better.

"I hope Sam's been a help," he offered, "she doesn't get to meet many young women."

"She?" Beverly turned her head to stare at Randall.

"I mean he," he countered, trying to cover his mistake.

She looked with renewed interest at Sam, who seemed to have ignored the statement. The lanky youth, the high voice, it all crystallized, "Sam's your daughter!"

"Quiet," Randall pleaded, "no one else knows. Please, I have to protect her, she wouldn't be safe."

"What do you mean?" asked Beverly.

"The King, he's a man of urges. He's likely to take her if he knows."

"Take her? She's just a child!"

"I wouldn't have a choice; he'd likely kill me."

"You fear him," she saw the look, "all of you. You only follow him because you're afraid of him. He's terrorized you into working for him."

Randall looked away in shame, "We need him, you see. He's the only thing keeping us alive. We didn't want to attack innocent people, but we have to survive."

"I understand now," said Beverly. "Tell me more about the Bandit King, Randall. Where's he from?"

"He came from up north. He was an archer in the king's army. Said he left the service to make more coins."

"So he's a deserter, then?"

"Maybe, but a more ruthless man you'll never meet. Everyone is afraid of him; he's a soldier, killed dozens of Norlanders and everything. We're just simple folk. We're no match for him."

"Does the King have an actual name?" she asked.

"Aye, he's called Lucas. Lucas Grumman, but he prefers to be called King."

"Will no one stand against him?" she asked.

"Once," he replied, "a man named Hanar did. The King took a liking to his wife, pretty young thing she was. When Hanar objected, Lucas struck him down; the man wasn't even armed! There was lots of complaints, but the King threatened to kill anyone who opposed him. Well, we was afraid, you see. None of us wanted to try to live off the land without help."

"That's irony," commented Beverly. "To think that farmers can't live off the land."

"I suppose it is," added Randall. "But farmers farm, not hunt. We don't know how to track animals or creep along silently."

"So how did you locate the King?" asked Beverly.

"Don't reckon I know. He'd already been in the area by the time I lost the farm. I heard from Josh Barnes about it. I'd gone to his house after being evicted. I hoped he could spare some food. Not that it did any good; the soldiers came for him the very next day. We were all in the same dire straits. We decided to head down this way to see if we could find the King. The winter was coming, you see, and starvation is a horrible way to die."

"I can imagine. So, aside from the King, no one here is a trained warrior?"

"No," he agreed. "We're just poor folk. It was either raid or starve."

"You could have made some bows?" she offered.

"No one here knows how. It was only after we took up with him that he started to show us. Even now, most of us are poor shots. I'd hate to think what I'd do if I was told to actually shoot someone."

"It's not an easy decision to take a man's life."

"True," the old man agreed, "but I feel so trapped. What else am I to do? If the earl sends a King's Ranger, we're all doomed. We'll be picked off one by one till we're all dead or wounded, and then those that are left alive will be hanged. The outlook is glum."

"Maybe not," added Beverly. "Things may yet turn out for the better."

Soon, they were all sitting around eating. The camp was eerily quiet, certainly not the camaraderie that she was used to from her days in Bodden. When the sky began to darken, each member of the gang left to take to their beds. Beverly was given a blanket, so she found a flat open space to lie down. It would be a fitful sleep, for she was still amongst bandits, but she was beginning to think there was little here to threaten her, save for the Bandit King himself.

Beverly awoke to the sound of chopping wood. It echoed throughout the clearing, bouncing off the trees like an eerie morning drum. She raised her head to see where the sound was coming from and spied Sam, her young hands trying unsuccessfully, to chop down a small tree. The axe was gripped awkwardly by the youth and each time she hit the trunk, the blade would slide off the bark, echoing each time.

Beverly rose to her feet, making her way towards the young girl. She was, perhaps, thirteen or so and Beverly was reminded of herself at her age. By then, of course, she had learned to use weapons, but Sam had difficulty with the simple task of holding a wood chopping axe.

Hearing her approach, a frustrated Sam turned, "It's not working!"

"You're holding it wrong," Beverly offered. "Let me show you," she said, taking the axe from the youngster's hands. "It's a two-handed axe, you need to hold it with your hands apart like so. Now, as you swing, you slide the other hand up the shaft, giving you more power." She swung the axe to demonstrate, and the blade bit into the wood. "There, you see?"

"Let me try," Sam begged.

Beverly stood by while the youngster tried the manoeuvre. "It's still not working!" she cried as the blade bounced off the bark, yet again.

"You have to keep the blade angled to the wood," Beverly offered. "Here, let me show you once more." She stood behind Sam, placing her hands over the young girl's, "Now, swing it slowly, and I'll guide you."

The two went through the motions and Sam smiled, "I see now. It's all about the grip."

"Yes, now you try it by yourself."

Sam swung the axe, and the tip chipped off a piece of bark.

"That's it," encouraged Beverly. "Try that a few more times, then start putting more weight behind it."

The axe was doing its work while Beverly watched with great interest as the young girl hacked away with considerable effort. Soon, Sam was breathing heavily and rubbing her arms. "It's a lot of work," she remarked.

"It takes years to build the muscles," explained Beverly. "Why don't you let me have a go for a while?" She took the offered axe and began cutting with strong, efficient strokes, soon to be rewarded with the tree splitting as its upper end fell to the forest floor. "There, you see? Now we have to chop it up for firewood."

They returned to the camp sometime later, carrying bundles of wood. Sam dropped hers by the fire and then sat down, tired from her exertions. Beverly, likewise, dropped hers, but noticed Randall across the clearing and made her way towards him.

"What are you up to this day?" she asked.

"What's that, Evelyn?"

"I was wondering what you're up to today. I thought we might make some better shelters."

"Oh yes, you'd mentioned that. Is it really worth the work?"

"Do you want to get wet when the water runs into your bed?" she asked.

"I suppose not. Couldn't we just move them?"

"We will, but there's more work to be done. I think it best if we remake them too."

"Why? Other than their position, what's wrong with them?" he asked.

"Where do I start?" she mused. "For one thing, they're facing the wrong way. The wind comes from the west here, right into the opening. You should angle them so that the opening points east. For another thing, the covering is very light. When it rains, I'm guessing the water leaks in, am I right?"

"Yes," he responded, dumbfounded. "How did you know that?"

She thought back to Gerald Matheson. He had shown her how to lead a patrol, and how to make a shelter as well as fight. She was about to say as much and then remembered where she was, "A wise man once told me. Now, what we need is thicker branches, with leaves on them. They'll cover the back of the lean-to and provide more proof against the rain. Of course, it would be better if you had full cover."

"Like the Bandit King?" suggested Randall.

"He has a tent, but there's no reason we couldn't build something better with a bit more time." She thought back to her days in Bodden and remembered her father moving the farmers closer to the Keep. It had taken months, and then the new houses had to be built. Her father had dug in and helped with the work himself. She could still remember him, covered in mud and dirt as he strode back into the Keep.

She was startled from her reverie by Randall, "You must have had quite the father, to teach you this. I wish I could do that for Sam."

"You have much you could teach, Randall. You're just down on your luck. Things will eventually improve, you have to believe that."

"I don't see much chance of that," he grumbled. "The only thing in my future is a noose. We all make our decisions in life and have to live with the consequences, I suppose."

"It doesn't have to be that way. What if I could find you a better solution?"

"What do you mean?"

"I don't know yet," she confessed, "but I have the beginnings of an idea. I'll let you know when I flesh it out."

Later in the morning, she spied an old woman struggling into camp, a bucket of water held in both hands as she strained to carry it. She set the bucket down and straightened, rubbing her back as she did so.

Beverly walked over to her. "May I help?" she offered.

"Oh, thank you," the woman replied. "That's most kind of you."

Beverly lifted the bucket, "I'm Evelyn, by the way."

"Agatha," the woman replied. "It's not the weight, it's just that my back gets sore from the strain."

"You need a yoke," Beverly suggested.

"A yoke?"

"Yes, a pole that sits across the shoulders. You hang buckets or baskets off of it, that way you can walk upright and not strain your back."

"Where would I get one of those?" the old woman queried.

"Someone here should be able to make one." Beverly looked around the camp as they walked, noticing a pile of goods. "What's that over there?"

"Those are things we took from the raids. There's all sorts of rubbish there. There's even some furniture, not that it's much use to us. Usually, we just end up burning it."

"I'll take a look," Beverly promised, "perhaps there's something useful in there. Is anyone here a carpenter?"

"No, but George over there can work with his hands. He made me a walking stick."

"Perfect, I'll go talk to him."

It didn't take long to produce a yoke. There was a long plank of wood that had been broken off of a crate, and then a notch was cut in it to set about a person's neck. George proved equal to the task, and a few hours later he had a workable solution.

Beverly and Agatha went down to the stream to try it out. There was no shortage of buckets here, for a raid on a merchant had produced an ample supply. Beverly loaded up two and slung them onto the yoke. Agatha stood beneath, and then straightened her back, raising the yoke on her shoulders. Beverly took two more buckets, using her hands to carry them. Soon, the two were back in camp, and there was sufficient water to allow Agatha a rest.

The afternoon wore on as Beverly roamed the camp. For a captive, she was shown remarkable freedom, but then again there was no place to go. Hearing a cry of alarm, she looked over to see a fox making off with a half-cooked rabbit. One of the bandits had been roasting it over a fire when the sneaky thief boldly ran up, grabbing it along with the skewer that had been holding it above the flames. The poor cook was livid, throwing sticks in the creature's direction, but to little effect. The man's meal disappeared into the woods, along with any hope of recovering it.

A small crowd gathered and were lamenting the loss as Beverly walked towards them. "Don't you post a watch?" she enquired.

"What was that?" asked the forlorn cook.

"You should post a watch. Have someone looking out for wild animals and such. Surely you have some older folk who could do such a thing, or perhaps a child? They only have to yell out if they see something."

"Hadn't thought of that," mused the cook. He turned to Randall who was amongst the crowd, "How about Sam? He could stand guard."

"Good idea," agreed Randall. "Sam, my boy, you wander around the camp watching the woods. If you see anything unusual, sing out."

"Yes, Father," Sam agreed. The youngster took her new task to heart, prowling the camp with a stern look.

It didn't take long for the new arrangement to bear fruit, for no sooner did a fresh rabbit hit the spit, than another fox appeared, likely drawn by the smell. Sam let out a yell, and soon the entire camp erupted into activity, bellows driving the startled creature away. Sam was pleased and beamed as the other folk congratulated her. She responded in as deep a voice as she could muster, still intent on maintaining her disguise.

The Bandit King erupted out of his tent, yelling at the crowd to shut up, his words slurred almost beyond recognition. He just as abruptly returned to his drinking after everyone quieted down. Beverly had been thinking that this evening might be an opportune time to confront him but decided it best to wait until he was no longer drunk.

She was looking over the pile of 'loot' that had been accumulated. There were baskets and crates, nails and even some cloth, though it was delicate, making it not suitable for shelters. The lace would have fetched a fair bit of coin, but it had been ruined by the weather, discarded in the bandits' ignorance.

She spotted Agatha sitting on a log and made her way over to her. "How's your back?" Beverly asked.

"Much better," the old woman replied. "And since I carried two buckets, I won't have to trek back down to the stream for some time."

"I'm surprised you didn't camp closer to the stream. It would have been easy for everyone to get their own water."

"It was the Bandit King's idea. He said this was a better position to defend."

Beverly looked around in surprise. She had spent her whole life training to be a warrior; she could see no advantage to this position whatsoever. She was beginning to suspect the Bandit King was less experienced than he claimed.

Soon, it grew dark and Agatha stood, "Must get these old bones off to bed, there'll be more work tomorrow. It never ends."

She started moving toward her ramshackle lean-to when Beverly called out. "Why don't you sleep in the wagon?" she asked.

Agatha turned, "Can't do that. His lordship don't like it."

"Where are all the other wagons?" Beverly asked.

"What other wagons?"

"I see mine, but surely there must have been others?"

"We used to take them up to Haverston, but then the locals started getting suspicious. These days we usually send them on their way without the cargo."

"But you didn't with me," stated Beverly. "Why is that?"

"I suspect the Bandit King took a liking to you. I'd watch him if I were you. Sooner or later he'll want you, and then it'll be all over."

"What's that mean?"

"It means what he wants, he gets. He's had his way with more than one woman in the past. Anyone who doesn't submit is banished. He's driven off most of the women, now it's just elderly folk like me. He's passed out from drink at the moment, but I'd hate to see you suffer the same fate."

"I'll bear that in mind," Beverly promised.

The bandits all retired for the night, and Beverly was surprised by the lack of organization. Though a person on watch had helped them during the day, nobody thought to take such precautions when the light faded. Beverly wandered the camp, deep in her thoughts. It would be so easy, she mused, to simply kill them all and eliminate the threat, but she knew she couldn't do it. These were simple folk, driven to their new life by terrible circumstances. There was no doubt in her mind that if she handed them over to the Earl of Shrewesdale, he would simply have them executed. She must find some way to save them. They were farmers, with useful skills, and if they had been near Bodden, they would have been welcomed with open arms. Her father's barony was always short of such skilled people, and she knew he would be thankful for having them, despite their story. It was at that precise moment that her plan crystallized. She would challenge the Bandit King for leadership of the small band and then kill him in single combat. She considered taking him into Shrewesdale alive, to face justice, but then he would talk, causing all these people to suffer. No, he had to die. Beverly was at peace with her decision.

Now that her mind was made up she needed to take action. It was too soon to challenge him. First, she must eliminate his hold over this group; make him look incompetent and less threatening. She needed to know more about the self-styled Bandit King, resolving to do so at the next opportunity.

Her mind now free from doubt, she settled down to sleep.

-Interlude VI-

BODDEN

Summer 960 MC

"So you became the Bandit Queen!" exclaimed Anna.

"No, Highness, that would be wrong," Beverly replied.

"Maybe," offered Hayley, "but it would make for an exciting story, nonetheless."

"I was there to stop the bandits, not lead them," Beverly pointed out.

"They're just egging you on, my dear," said the Baron.

"Well, tell us the rest," demanded Gerald. "You've peaked our interest."

"I will," she replied, "but first, tell me what you would've done? Let's start with you, Gerald.

Gerald thought about it a moment before replying, "I suppose I would have killed the Bandit King outright and told the farmers to get lost."

"And leave them to their fate?" asked Hayley. "That wouldn't do. It wasn't their fault they were bandits, the earl drove them to it."

"They still broke the law," commented the baron. "It is the duty of a knight to follow the wishes of their master."

"Yes," agreed Hayley, "but surely injustice must be fought when necessary?"

"It seems," offered Gerald, "that we do not all agree on the task at hand. I'm curious to see how you handled it, aren't you, my lord?"

"I'm afraid I cannot comment on the matter as I already know the result," the baron admitted.

"How is that even fair?" complained the princess. "You must tell us how she resolved it."

"I believe that is Beverly's duty," Fitz said, sipping some wine. "She'll tell it from her point of view, and there's still some details I'm not aware of."

"Well for Saxnor's sake," complained Hayley, "get on with the story, Beverly, we're all holding our breath!"

Beverly smiled at the ranger's look of eagerness, "Very well, I shall continue. Now, where was I?"

"You had just decided to find out more about the Bandit King before you took over," offered Anna.

"Oh yes, that's right…"

Beverly and the Bandit King: Part III

Summer 955 MC

The next morning, the Bandit King and the men went out to watch the road for merchants. Beverly took it upon herself to organize things. She retrieved a barrel from the raider spoils, setting it upright in the middle of camp. The women then filled it with water from the stream to create a reservoir. Next, she set them to task taking apart the crude shelters they had been using. Organizing them into teams, she had some gathering sticks for the new construction, while others removed the old. They were willing accomplices and seemed to flourish under her guidance. By noon, the beginnings of a decent encampment was built before they sat by the fire for a rest.

"What do you know about the Bandit King?" Beverly asked.

"He's a soldier," said Agatha. "Come from up north."

"Yes," agreed Beverly, "Randall said as much, but is there anything else you can tell me about him?"

"He has a fine sword," offered a woman named Grace. "I've seen him with it."

"I reckon he stole it," added Agatha. "He waves it around quite a bit, but I don't think he knows how to handle it."

"My Tom," commented Grace, "says he's never seen him use it."

"Perhaps he's a bowman," suggested Beverly. "He appears to have the arms for it."

"I seen him use the bow once," recollected Grace, "killed a hare at thirty paces."

"Why don't you go peek in his tent?" suggested Agatha. "It's not as if any of us'll say anything."

"I think I will," decided Beverly, rising to her feet.

She walked over to the tent, moving the flap to peer inside. It was a small enclosure, and she had to crouch to enter. The simple structure had furs laid out like a rug, obviously a prize that had been taken on the road. More piles of furs lay beside the bed, but little else was present. She rummaged through the pile, discovering a box within. It was a strongbox made of metal, though the hasp was damaged, likely from a hammer or the hilt of a sword smashing it open. Inside she found a significant number of coins, but the real prize came at the bottom, for there she found an old document. It was folded many times, and she carefully removed it, holding it up as she examined it.

It was a soldier's contract. It bore the name of Lucas Grumman and indicated he was part of the Kingsford archers. She placed everything back to where she had found it and returned to the fire.

"He's a common bowman, I saw his contract. I suspect he's lying to you about his service. The Kingsford archers haven't been anywhere near the northern border. I doubt he's seen any real battles."

"You mean he's not a warrior?" asked Agatha.

"He's a soldier, but likely an untried one. I shall see if I can learn more over the next day or so. Has he handed out your share of the loot?"

"We don't get any coin," muttered Grace. "He says it's what we owe him for leading us."

"Does he, now? That hardly seems fair."

She looked up at the sky to judge the time and decided it would be best get back to work. The men would likely be returning soon, and she wanted the new shelters built before the others arrived.

The men returned late in the afternoon, wearing long faces. All day had been spent waiting for prey, only to be left empty-handed, for no wagons travelled the road. The sight of the new, sturdier shelters was a pleasant distraction for the dejected returnees. Soon, the camp was abuzz with chatter as the women explained what had happened. The Bandit King, in a foul mood, turned without any comment, disappearing into his tent.

Agatha turned to Beverly, "You'd best get into the woods," she said. "And be quick about it. The King is in one of his moods, and I fear he may decide to have you."

Beverly made to protest, but the woman was insistent, so she entered the underbrush, concealing herself from the camp. Through the branches, she watched to see what would transpire.

The Bandit King wandered out of his tent. "Bring me the redhead," he bellowed.

It was Agatha who spoke up, "Can't" she yelled.

"What d'you mean, 'Can't'?" he slurred.

"She's got the cramps."

The bandit leader wore a puzzled expression.

"She's bleeding, it's her time," Agatha persisted.

The man swore in disgust and re-entered his tent, cursing some more, and then a bottle flew from the tent flap to smash harmlessly on the ground. A short time later snoring was heard coming from the drunken Bandit King's tent.

Agatha motioned for Beverly to return.

"Is it always like this?" she asked the old woman.

"It is, if the woman is young. You're safe for now, he'll be asleep till dawn."

With their leader retired, the rest of the camp seemed almost festive. Although they had failed to find any loot, the new sleeping arrangements lightened everyone's mood.

Beverly awoke before dawn, as years of heading out on patrols caused her to rise early, and today was no different. Watching the leader's tent, she waited for him to rise. Sure enough, the flap opened and out he came, wandering across the camp. He entered the edge of the wood, likely intent on a morning piss.

Dame Beverly followed at a discreet distance, hoping to get the chance to finally finish him off. She had pulled her dagger and moved forward to complete her task when he stopped in a small clearing as she had expected him to do so. Indeed, she was ready to spring into action the moment he started his business, but what he did next took her by surprise. He bent down, moved a rock and pulled forth a folded paper. She couldn't make out what was on it, but it didn't matter for the Bandit King tossed it aside after reading it, and then headed back to the camp.

Beverly waited until he had left the area to retrieve the paper. It was a handwritten note which simply stated, 'a rich merchant has left the Shepherd's Tavern on the Shrewesdale road this morning'. She remembered the tavern, for it was one of several such establishments that existed along the king's road, typically a day's travel apart. It appeared that someone at the tavern was tipping off the bandits!

She kept the note, tucking it into her dress, and returned to camp to see the men assembling once more. The Bandit King left for the road, and this time, Beverly followed. Arriving at the ambush point, their leader saw fit to line them up. Beverly was shocked to see his lack of experience, for the Bandit King placed archers on both sides of the road. If even one shot at a target and missed, there was a very real chance they might hit their own men.

Resolving to stop the attack before it could commence, she edged around the perimeter of the ambush and began travelling north on the road. It didn't take long for her to locate the merchant. He was driving a team of two horses who pulled a rather sturdy looking wagon. She stood in the middle of the road, holding up her hand and the horses came to rest just in front of her.

"Is there a problem, miss?" the man cried out.

"I'm here to warn you, sir," she replied. "There are bandits up ahead, and they mean you harm."

"Are you all right?" he asked. "Do you need assistance?"

"No, I'm fine," she said. "You must turn back or risk your life. I suggest you return to the Shepherd's Tavern and stay there till a patrol of knights arrives."

"Knights?" the merchant asked.

"Yes, knights from Shrewesdale frequent this road every few days. I'm sure they would be more than willing to escort you to the city in safety, should you ask."

"I must thank you," the trader said, "but surely you are in need of assistance?"

"No, I'm fine, thank you anyways. Should you see the knights, please tell Sir Heward that Dame Beverly says hello." She smiled at the thought. What would The Axe make of it, she wondered?

The merchant turned around, leading his wagon off to the safety of the north. Beverly returned to the camp; the Bandit King would be denied his prey this day.

Back in the camp, she was secure in the knowledge that the bandits would wait for some time before finally coming to the conclusion that the wagon would not be arriving. Making her way to the leader's tent, she retrieved the coins that he had stashed there. If things went her way, this would be the final straw that broke the donkey's back. Now all she had to do was wait.

The group finally returned, grumbling as they walked. The Bandit King did not look pleased, and he stared at her as he entered the camp. This time she met his gaze with an unwavering look. He seemed startled by her response and looked away, berating someone nearby for not doing their job. He stalked across the clearing and disappeared into his tent.

Beverly called the men over and starting distributing coins.

"What's this?" asked Randall.

"Your share of the past raids. The Bandit King surely has no need of this much coin, he's been hoarding it for months. You deserve to celebrate, don't you think?"

"And how would we do that?" he asked.

"Didn't your leader tell you?" she returned. "There's an inn just down the road, to the north. It's called the Shepherd's Tavern. You can probably walk there without too much trouble. You could buy some food and still have leftover coin."

The men started grumbling. Randall was about to ask something, but a yell from the Bandit King's tent drew their attention. He emerged, staring daggers at those around him. "Who went in my tent?" he yelled. "Who's taken my coin?"

"I did," Beverly said calmly, "and I gave it to the men."

"What's the meaning of this?" he bellowed.

"I've decided that I'm going to take over this band. You're doing a rat's ass job of it."

The Bandit King drew his sword and starting running toward her, rage contorting his face. Beverly lifted the hem of her dress and drew her dagger. She easily sidestepped his clumsy strike, while he barreled past her.

"Who do you think you are?" he yelled, wheeling on her.

"I'm Dame Beverly Fitzwilliam," she announced, "Knight of the Sword. You're no Bandit King, you're a filthy deserter! Surrender yourself and face the penalty for your crimes."

There was murmuring all about the camp as the bandits began to gather to watch the confrontation.

"I choose death," he snarled, "yours to be precise." He struck again with the blade, and Beverly parried with her dagger.

"Impressive," he said, "you're quick, I'll give you that, but it won't help you. I've killed more men than I can count. Prepare for your death, Dame Beverly. I won't promise it'll be quick, but it will be fun, at least for me."

Beverly backed up, keeping her eyes on him. She felt vulnerable without her armour, so she crouched and began cutting the hem of her skirt.

"Go ahead," he mocked, "take your time."

She cut the cloth from her hem, then called Randall over. "Tie this around my wrist," she asked, "it'll give me some protection." Randall did as she asked, and when he was finished she beckoned her opponent, "Come along, let's get this over with."

He launched himself at her, while she parried his attack, stepping back slightly. The deserter repeated his action. She now had a good idea of his capabilities, based upon the predictability of his attacks. She remembered back to all the training she had received as a young woman and pledged to thank Gerald for his lessons. She was certain she could beat him, but the problem was his advantage in reach, for his sword was superior to her dagger in this regard. Somehow, she needed to get within his range before she could attack.

She stepped back each time he struck, drawing him in, as she parried each strike. Soon, she was near the fire pit, and she sank her foot into the ash. As he commenced his next attack, she parried, and then kicked with her foot, sending ash into the man's face. Her target staggered backwards, and she leaped forward, grappling with him. She intended to subdue him, to bring him to justice, but he proved to be too strong. The two combatants fell to the ground in a heap, but just as they landed, the Bandit King managed to flip her, leaving her prone on her back. Her dagger had flown from her hand, and now his body straddled hers. He raised his arms above her, lifting his blade for the killing blow, then suddenly he screamed in pain, falling to the side.

Reacting quickly to this sudden turn of events, she rolled away from him, grasping her dagger which had fallen just out of reach. She rose to a crouching position while he cursed, an arrow protruding from his side. He pulled it out with his left hand, grimacing as he did so, looking to his assailant. There was young Sam, holding the bow and Beverly knew the youth would be his next target. She sprang forward, driving the dagger into the man's chest, hearing bone snap as she pushed with all her might. The Bandit King dropped, unmoving, the life gone from his body. She rose to her feet, not quite believing the turn of events. Glancing around at the people watching her she beheld the look of shock evident on their faces.

"This man," she proclaimed, "has suffered the King's Justice and has been punished for his crimes."

It was Randall who stepped forward first, "We surrender to you, Dame Beverly. We will confess our crimes and submit to the King's Justice."

It was done, she had performed her duty. All she had to do was return to Shrewesdale with the Bandit King's body and turn over the prisoners, and yet she couldn't bring herself to do it. These people had suffered injustice; she could not punish them under these circumstances.

"No," she announced, "I will not arrest you. You had little choice in this. I have the body of the Bandit King. That will suffice."

"But what will we do? We're all doomed."

"No," she said, "you're not. Tell me, Randall, if you had a chance to start over, under a fair and just noble, would you make the best of your opportunity?"

"Of course," he replied, "as would we all. What are you saying?"

"You're decent people," she continued, "and you deserve a second chance. My father is the Baron of Bodden, and is always short of farmers. Make your way there, and he will grant you land."

"Why would he do that? He doesn't know us?"

"I will give you a letter of introduction, in my own hand. I'm sure there's more than enough coin to get you all to Bodden. You can take my wagon and horses."

Beverly was not surprised to see the look of relief on the faces of the crowd. They were farmers, not bandits, and the earl had robbed them of their livelihood. She was only setting things right.

It didn't take much time to gather the group's meager belongings. She helped them load up the wagon, and then they transported her to the road, along with the body of their leader. She watched the wagons disappear as they made their way north on the road. Confident she had done the right thing, she started heading south, carrying the body on her shoulders. It didn't take long before she saw the dust cloud as a patrol of knights came into view.

-Interlude VII-

BODDEN

Summer 960 MC

"Well, that explains a lot," said the Baron. "I never did figure out how you met them, but, quite frankly, I didn't care. We can always use extra farmers here."

Beverly smiled, "I knew you'd welcome them father, and I thought you wouldn't need to know their background."

"Well," he admitted, "I suspect if I'd known, I might have chosen differently, but I must say they've worked out well. That youngster, Samantha, she's taken up the bow and I've had her trained as an archer."

"It isn't the first time you've had a woman in your army, Lord," said Gerald, grinning from ear to ear.

"Good point, Gerald, though I daresay I'm getting a little old for this."

"Didn't you run into problems with the knights?" asked Hayley. "I would have thought they'd just take the credit."

"And well they might of," said Beverly, "but as chance would have it, the patrol was led by none other than Sir Heward himself. He insisted on me getting the recognition, though to be fair I didn't really care. I took care of the problem, and the countess was ecstatic."

"I bet," said Anna, "that she didn't let the earl forget it."

"No," said Beverly, "though unfortunately, when she died, everything changed."

Beverly fell silent and the others, in understanding, remained quiet.

A servant opened the door for Lady Albreda, who entered the room. Her hair was in the long braid for which she was well known, but today she wore a pale blue dress which seemed to make her glide across the floor. "Greetings, all," she offered as she halted beside Fitz, placing her hand on his shoulder while she took in the scene. "What do we have here?"

"We're telling stories," explained Anna.

"Yes," added Gerald. "Beverly was just telling us about the Bandit King, a fascinating tale."

"Interesting," Albreda observed, "and whose turn is it now?"

Fitz lifted his hand to his shoulder, touching hers, "We were just about to decide that."

"Somebody else must have a story," said Anna.

"Perhaps," offered Albreda, "Hayley would like to tell her tale."

The ranger sat up in surprise, "Me? I don't have a story."

"That's not what I've heard," said Albreda. "Why don't you tell everyone about the Beast of Mattingly?"

Hayley looked dumbfounded, "How do you know about that?"

"I hear things," said Albreda. "Now come, tell us all about it."

"Yes. Tell us, Hayley," begged Anna, "we need another story."

"All right. Let's see, where do I start?"

"When did it take place?" asked Anna.

"Just after I won the archery competition in Uxley, back in 958."

"Summer of 958," corrected Gerald.

"Yes, summer of '58, the morning after I beat Ranger Osferth. Whatever happened to him, by the way?"

"He died," said Gerald, "or so I heard. Unfortunate, but don't let it interrupt your story."

"Right," agreed Hayley, "anyways, there I was getting ready to leave Uxley…"

Hayley and the Beast: Part I

THE KINGS ROAD

Summer 958 MC

Hayley Chambers rolled over in the bed, for it wasn't often that she had the opportunity to sleep on a mattress, and she was determined to get her coin's worth. The sun had other ideas, however, and insisted on peeking through the shutters, flooding across her face, forcing her to move. She pulled the pillow over her head in a vain effort to block the sun, but the damage was already done; she was wide awake.

Rising to a sitting position, she cast her eyes around the room. It took her a moment to get her bearings, for she had spent the previous night celebrating. Uxley; that was it. The Old Oak Tavern. Her memories came flooding back; the archery competition, the festivities, the endless rounds of drinks. She wiped the hair from her face and dropped her legs over the side of the bed. She was dying of thirst and moved to the small bowl resting on the table nearby to splash her face.

Her stomach growled, and she realized how hungry she was. Dressing quickly, she tied her hair back into its customary ponytail, and then made her way downstairs to the common room. The place was mostly deserted, save for a barmaid wiping down the tables. There was a quick hello, but Hayley's mind was still fogged from the hangover, and she stumbled into a chair at the nearest table.

"Can I get you some food, love?" asked the barmaid. "You look like you need it."

Hayley cast her blurry eyes in the woman's direction, "Yes, please, and something to drink, my throat is raw."

"I'll get you some cider," the barmaid replied, "and we've got some nice porridge on the go."

"Excellent," Hayley replied, then fell silent.

A short time later she was digging in, and as the breakfast made its way to her stomach, she began to feel better.

Arlo Harris, the owner and barkeep, came out of the back room and nodded in her direction. "Morning," he said.

Hayley stopped eating to take a drink, "Is the other ranger about?" She seemed to remember beating him in the archery competition, but couldn't remember the details.

"'Fraid not, miss," Arlo replied. "He left at sun up."

"Sun up? What time is it now?"

"Mid-morning," he replied.

Hayley stared at him for a moment, trying to remember last evening's activities, "How did I get to bed last night?"

"You were carried. You passed out in the room, here. Little worse for the wear, are we?" he chuckled.

"I've had worse," she admitted. "The other ranger, the fellow with the red hair, what was his name?"

"Osferth, miss."

"Yes, Osferth. What kind of mood was he in when he left?"

"A foul one. You trounced him thoroughly in the tournament. I don't think he's gonna to forget you anytime soon."

"Which way did he head?" she asked.

"North, at first light, why?"

"I didn't want to run into him on the road, but I'm heading north, too."

"Why north?" he asked. "I thought the rangers patrolled all the roads."

"True, but the people up north need more help dealing with wild animals."

"I thought you patrolled the roads, locked up bandits and such?"

"We do, but I prefer tracking animals."

"I take it you hunt a lot?"

"Not really. I only hunt when I need to, but I find animals fascinating. I like observing them and learning more about them. I once tracked a pack of wolves for over a week!"

"The only good wolf is a dead wolf," the barkeep scoffed. "If you don't mind me saying, the very idea of watching them seems absurd."

"I don't mind," she responded. "I know it sounds strange, but I've learned lots about them. It'll make it easier in the future if I have to deal with them."

She polished off her cider and stood, straightening her belt while she fished for her coin purse.

"There's no need for that," Arlo objected, "you're a King's Ranger."

"Nonsense," she insisted, pulling out some coins. "I've got the coin, what else am I to do with it other than spend it!"

The rhythmic swaying of her horse had a soporific effect on Hayley Chambers as she thought of how to spend her winnings. She imagined herself at a luxurious inn, with a hot bath and a fancy meal. Perhaps she'd dazzle a young lord and be swept off her feet. She knew this to be unlikely, for the nobles in this part of the country were either far too young, or obnoxious. She wondered if perhaps there were only those two stages of noble life. It must be nice to live a life of luxury and not have to work for a living.

The road up ahead entered some woods, and she watched for low hanging branches. It wouldn't be the first time she'd hit her head for not paying attention, and she knew it likely would not be the last. She must stop her daydreaming and return to the task at hand.

The road meandered for some time, likely it followed an old path, clear of trees and roots. She heard a noise up ahead and slowed her pace, lest there be bandits in the area. As she rounded the corner, she saw a man hanging from a tree. There was a woman and two children trying to cut him down, but it was obvious the man was dead, for he was not moving. The rope around his neck was fashioned into a hangman's noose, and she knew immediately that this must be the work of the ranger Osferth, for who else but a King's Ranger would carry out such summary justice.

At the sound of her approach, the woman turned and let out a shout of alarm. Into the woods the children scuttled, their mother just behind them.

Hayley rode up to the body to examine it. She pressed the flesh of the hand, and it turned white, the blood not returning. She concluded the man had been killed quite recently for there was no sign yet of the hardening of the body that occurred after death. A torn piece of parchment was attached to the man's chest by a nail, and Hayley removed it to read the word 'poacher' written on it in rough letters. So, she thought, Osferth managed to find himself a criminal to vent his frustrations on.

Thoroughly disgusted by the act, Hayley resolved to cut the man down from the tree. She hauled a rope from the back of her saddle and lashed it to the poor victim, then looped it over the branch, tying the ends to her saddle. From her present position, she was just high enough to stand on her horse and start cutting the noose he hung from. As the strands parted, her own rope took up the weight, then, with a final sawing motion, the old rope broke, and she lowered the body to the ground.

She saw the woman, watching from the edge of the woods and called out to her, "Come out, I mean you no harm."

"It's against the law to cut down a poacher," she called back.

"I'm a King's Ranger, it's all right. Did you see the man that did this?"

"Yes, a man with red hair," the woman cried out.

"I've cut him down so you can bury him," Hayley offered. "The man you described is on the way north. He won't be back here for many a week. Your husband needs a proper burial. Do you need help?"

"No," the woman responded from the safety of the wood. "I'll see to it."

"How will you survive without your husband?" asked the ranger.

"I'll make do, never you mind." The woman emerged from the tree line, and Hayley observed her attire. She must be living rough, for her clothes were bedraggled and her hair a tangled mess.

It only took Hayley a moment to make up her mind. "Very well," she said, "I'll leave you to it." As the woman drew closer, Hayley tossed the pouch to her, "You might as well have this. I'd only waste it anyway."

The woman caught the purse and looked at it in surprise, asking "Who are you?"

"Ranger Hayley Chambers," she replied. "Now I must be off. Good luck to you!" She turned her horse and resumed her journey north. Ah well, she thought, the widow has more need of the coin than I.

A few days later she was topping the hill overlooking Tewsbury, its chimney's smoking as the commoners prepared their evening meals. Every major city in the kingdom housed a tavern called the King's Arms. Owned by the crown, the alehouses had been built to accommodate the King's Rangers when needed, and also doubled as a drop point for messages. Hayley knew there weren't many rangers left these days. Rumours were that the king was less than happy with the constant drain on the royal purse.

Being familiar with the town, she made her way directly to the tavern, leaving her mount at the stables. Inside, she saw the old, familiar face of Langston at the bar.

"Hayley," the old man greeted her, "back so soon? I'd have thought you'd be in the capital by now."

"Changed my mind," she replied. "There's too much politics in Wincaster. I'm a simple country girl."

Langston poured her an ale, setting it down on the counter in front of her. "Here," he said, "wet your whistle." He watched her as she took a pull of the strong drink, "Well, what d'ya think?"

"Hmmm," she replied, "it's nice. You've added something to it; it's very tasty."

The bartender beamed, "Honey. Makes it smoother. Took me weeks to find the right balance."

"Well," she mused, "this is definitely something to keep on the menu." She took another sip, letting the smooth liquid coat her throat. She had never realized how thirsty one could get travelling the roads. "Any news?" she asked.

Langston turned to the wall behind him, grabbing a small wooden box. "Let me see," he said, opening it. He withdrew a parchment, unrolling it on the counter in front of her. "There seems to be a problem out Mattingly way," he said, rotating the paper for her to see.

Hayley looked down at the note; its precise hand easy to read. "Appears something's attacking the livestock," she said.

"Looks like a job for a ranger," commented the barkeep. "Think you're up to it?"

"I suppose I better be," she replied, "unless you know of another ranger in the area?"

"'Fraid not," the man replied. "I saw Wilson, but he's on his way out to Kingsford, left three days ago."

"I didn't see him on the road," remarked Hayley.

"I don't suppose you would have. He's heading west, on the Bodden road, then south through Redridge."

"Problems in Kingsford?"

"No," replied Langston, "but he's got family in the city, probably wants to see them."

"Did a ranger named Osferth travel through? He was half a day ahead of me."

"I 'aven't seen him if he did. The place has been dead quiet. Why d'you ask?"

"He hanged a poacher on the road, a few days back. I just wanted to hear his side of the story."

"Well," continued Langston, "poaching has been on the rise the last few years. Strange that."

"Not so strange, my friend," offered Hayley. "It wasn't that long ago that all the free land was claimed by the crown. In my grandfather's day, there was no poaching, only hunting. Now, only the nobles hunt freely."

"And the rangers," reminded the barkeep.

"True," she replied. "My own father was hanged for poaching. Too bad he wasn't a ranger. Which reminds me, I've a small deer that I wandered across on the way into town. I don't suppose you might be able to make use of it?"

Langston smiled, displaying his rotting teeth, "Oh, I think I can find a home for it in my fireplace, don't you worry. I'll have someone go fetch it, shall I?"

"I'd be obliged," she said.

"Will you be heading straight out?" he asked.

"No, I'll spend the night and head out in the morning. Can't let you have all that venison to yourself, now can I?"

Three days later, Hayley rode into Mattingly. It was a small village, astride the upper reaches of the Alde River. In times past the king had placed a garrison here to guard the ford, but these days, this part of the frontier was generally quiet, and the king had withdrawn the garrison back to Tewsbury. The village was little more than a small group of buildings clustered around the Green Unicorn, the local tavern. It was here that Hayley decided to visit first, for surely it was the hub of the village.

She tied her horse to a tree outside and made her way into the structure, to be greeted by a sudden increase in the noise level. The place was busy and the din of voices almost overwhelming. She pushed her way through the crowd to the bar to see an old man with a wispy grey beard and sideburns pouring ale for the local smith, judging by the look of his hands.

"What can I get you, miss?" the man asked.

"A mug of ale, if you please," she said, tossing some coins onto the bar. "Is it always so busy here?"

The barkeep poured the ale and deposited it in front of her before answering, "Not usually, but the town has gathered to talk about the attacks."

"I heard something about those," she commented. "Can you tell me more?"

"There's been some cattle killed and stolen," he said as if that was all the explanation that was necessary.

"Killed and stolen? How do you know it was killed if it was stolen?"

"Don't be a smartass," the man chided. "Some cows were killed, and others were carted off."

"So there's thieves or bandits in the area?"

"No, an animal of some sort. I've heard that it's got big claws and tore a cow to bits. What's it to you?"

"Actually," she admitted, "I've been sent here to investigate. I'm a King's Ranger."

The man stared at her in disbelief, "You're a King's Ranger? Don't make me laugh!" Despite his words to the contrary, he started laughing, a deep belly full of chuckles that seemed contagious to Hayley, for she was soon joining in.

He finally stopped, wiping a tear from his eye with his apron. "That's a good one," he said. "You had me going for a moment."

She pulled the ranger's medallion from her neck. Each King's Ranger had one with the royal crest of the order on one side, and the ranger's number on the reverse. If two rangers should meet, the lower number was always considered the senior. She held the medallion up before the barkeep, "See? I actually am a ranger!"

The look of shock on the man's face was priceless, and Hayley smiled, batting her eyelashes at him.

"Saxnor's balls, I've never heard of a woman being a ranger before."

"You should get around more," she offered. "There's more of us than you might think." She was casting her eyes about the crowd as she talked, "Who's in charge around here?"

The barkeep pointed across the room, "See that man over there? The one with the bald head and the moustache? His name's Simon Agramont. He's the one you want to talk to."

"Is he the mayor?" she asked.

"Mayor? No, we're not big enough for one of those. He's the reeve. He manages the village on behalf of the Earl of Tewsbury."

"Thank you," she said, downing her ale in one large pull. She wiped her mouth on her sleeve and then began making her way through the crowd once more. As she got closer to her target, she heard him talking to his companion, a man who looked like a farmer of sorts.

"I tell you, Andrew, the earl has sent for a ranger. Once he gets here, he can track the beast down. We're not going to send a bunch of farmers into the woods on a wild goose chase. It could be dangerous."

The man he was talking to was obviously not happy with the delay and turned away in disgust, heading for the bar.

Hayley took the opportunity to introduce herself. "Reeve Agramont?" she asked.

He turned at the mention of his name, "Is there something I can help you with?"

"Actually, I think there's something I can help you with," she said. "I'm Hayley Chambers. I've been sent by the King's Rangers to investigate this problem of yours."

"It's about time you got here," the man sneered. "We asked for a ranger weeks ago."

"Sorry, but the rangers have been stretched to the limit of late," answered Hayley. "What can you tell me about the attacks?"

"They've been going on since the winter thaw. Something's been killing the cattle."

"Can you show me where?" she asked.

"Yes, of course," he replied. He was about to move towards the door and then stopped suddenly. "Are you sure you're up to this? You look a little young."

"Trust me," she said, "I've been tracking all my life. My father said I was tracking before I was walking."

The reeve didn't seem impressed by her bravado, despite Hayley's best smile.

"Follow me," the man said glumly, leading her toward the exit. "The latest attack was last night, to the south of town. The farm is only a short distance away."

"Wolves?" she asked.

"No," he denied, "definitely not. You'll see what I mean when we get there."

It took some time to arrive at the pasture. Hayley looked up at the sky; daylight wouldn't last much longer. She dismounted and followed Simon to where the carcass was. It lay there in a pool of blood, with large claw marks raked across the creature's belly.

"Interesting," she commented.

"Can you tell what did it?" Simon asked.

"Certainly not a wolf," she agreed.

The man snorted in disgust, "I knew that. Did you come here only to tell me what I already know?"

Hayley ignored the man's belligerence, "The claw marks are large, not those of a wild cat or even bear." She bent down to examine the carcass in more detail. "There's another wound up here by the neck."

Simon looked surprised at her discovery. "Can you tell what killed it?" he asked.

"Something big. It appears to have snapped the cow's neck. It would take some strength to do that." She stood up, casting her eyes about the field, "Have the remains been moved at all?"

"No, of course not, who'd want to move this?" he said, gesturing with his hands.

Hayley again ignored the man's behaviour and started wandering about, her eyes scanning the ground for details.

"Find any tracks?" the man asked.

"A few, but they just disappear. It looks like something big attacked the cows. How many cattle were here?"

"Farmer Hayes said there were twelve."

She scanned the field. "One's been taken," she remarked.

"Yes," agreed Simon, "a calf. Surely you can track it?"

"No," she answered. "Though I can tell where it was killed."

The villager began to get agitated. "Are you telling me," he said, "that you can't even track a cow? I thought you were a King's Ranger?"

Hayley rose from where she was examining the tracks, "I can assure you; I AM a King's Ranger. I'll investigate this problem of yours, I promise you. In the meantime, let me see to this uninterrupted. You'd best head back to the village, and I'll continue to look around, but it'll take some time. If I find anything, I'll be sure to let you know."

The reeve left without comment, beginning the walk back into the village, grumbling as he did so.

Hayley was baffled. She saw the pool of blood on the ground where the calf had been killed, but couldn't for the life of her figure out what had happened. She walked around the stain on the grass, looking for any signs of tracks. She finally came across a single print. Bending closer, she observed a strange depression. It appeared to be a three-toed print, with deeper cuts at the end, most likely talons. She wondered if this was some type of giant eagle or falcon, but the mark was far too large for any such creature.

She stood, surveying the surrounding terrain. If something had carried off the carcass, it would be impossible to track. How would she proceed? She stared back at the ground; surely if this much blood was spilled, the body must have been dripping. Perhaps she could find a trail?

It would be a monumentally difficult task, but she had to act quickly, for soon it would be dark, and the trail would be impossible to locate. She crawled around the scene of the slaughter, examining the ground in minute detail, looking for any signs of a trail. Sure enough, just as the sun was starting to set, she found what she was looking for; a small spattering of blood a fair distance from the killing. She marked it with a stick and then rose to look back at the scene of the attack. Letting her eyes follow the line from larger blood pool, to her present location, she turned, extending her gaze in the same direction, eastward. Of course, the creature might have circled the area, but she thought that unlikely. Chances were, with a heavy load, the attacker would want to get away as quickly as possible to devour their prey.

She looked to the trees in the distance, the setting sun casting its last light across the sky, illuminating the treetops with a golden glow just before it sank beyond the horizon. In that briefest of moments, she saw a single pine tree, its top broken near the tip. Was this a clue? Knowing it would be too dark to proceed, she lined up two sticks by pushing them into the ground, forming a line pointing at the broken tree. Now, when morning came, she would be able to head toward the mysterious tree in the distance.

As a ranger, she was used to sleeping outdoors, and so she lit a fire and rolled out her blanket, settling in for the night. The morning sun rose to find her packed and ready to begin her trek. It took some time to reach the broken tree and then came the difficult task of climbing it. Many scrapes and cuts later, she was precariously perched near the top branch, the treetop swaying unsteadily as her weight shifted. Examining the break in more detail, she realized the snapped off top held no clues, and she was disheartened that her efforts had proven futile. Admitting defeat, she began climbing back down, when something caught her eye. Wedged in among the pine needles was a feather. She reached out to carefully grasp it, tucking the large brown plume securely into her tunic before continuing her descent. Perhaps now she could uncover what this creature was.

Once she returned to Mattingly, she spared no time tracking down the reeve. He was sitting out front of his home, watching the passers-by as she approached.

"Back so soon?" he asked.

"I've found something," she said, "but I need help to figure out what it means."

"What is it?"

She pulled the unusually large feather from beneath her tunic. "This," she said. "Have you any idea what it is?"

"It's just a feather," he said. "Stop wasting my time. You need to get back out there and follow whatever trail you can find."

"Do you know what type of feather it is?" she asked.

"How should I know," was the retort. "I don't know the first thing about birds, isn't that your job?"

"Is there anyone around who might be able to help me? It's important. It may lead to a clue concerning our mysterious visitor."

The reeve pursed his lips as he thought, "You might try the old hermit, goes by the name Aldus Hearn. He knows all kinds of things about the creatures in these parts."

"And where do I find him?" she asked, her curiosity peaked.

"He lives in an old shack to the southeast of town, up near the edge of the wood. You'll know it when you see it."

She nodded her thanks and set forth to find this mysterious hermit.

-Interlude VIII-

BODDEN

Summer 960 MC

"Did you have any idea what it was at this time?" asked the baron.

"Well, naturally I thought it was a giant bird," offered the ranger.

"Are there really birds that large?" asked Beverly.

"Why wouldn't there be?" answered Albreda, in response. "Do you think that only mammals grow large?"

"I've never seen a giant bird before," explained Beverly.

"And I've never seen a ship. But just because I haven't seen one doesn't mean they don't exist."

"I see your point," offered Beverly.

"You're the Druid," commented the baron. "Do you have giant birds in the Whitewood?"

She smiled mysteriously, "Perhaps you'll come visit and see for yourself. The Whitewood holds all kinds of mysteries."

"I look forward to it," offered the baron.

"Can we please get back on track here," insisted the princess. "You two can make eyes later, when the tales are done."

"Make eyes?" said Fitz in surprise.

"You know what I mean," said Anna. "No offence intended."

"I must protest," said Albreda, "I think you're misinterpreting my intentions."

"Is she?" the baron asked, turning to the Druid.

Albreda blushed, "No, she's not, but perhaps there's a better time and place to talk about this."

The baron cleared his throat, "Yes, by all means. Now, back to the story. You were on your way to see this Aldus Hearn person."

"Yes, that's right," said Hayley, "on the outskirts of Mattingly...."

Hayley and the Beast Part: II

Summer 958 MC

T he directions were somewhat imprecise, and it took some time to finally locate the man's abode, but now, as she stood before it, she wondered if she had made a mistake.

It was a wooden structure with walls of mud lathered over some type of frame, which could be seen through holes where the mud had fallen off. The cedar shingle roof appeared to be in the same state of disrepair, and she wondered how it would ever protect anything from the rain. The structure looked abandoned, as if it hadn't been used in years. There was no door, only a leather skin covering the entryway which she approached with trepidation.

"Hello," she called out, "is anyone home?" There was no answer, and so she moved closer, knocking on the frame of the doorway, "Hello?"

Hearing a rustling behind her, she turned to see a man approaching from the forest. His long brown robe was tattered at the edges and seemed to be in the same state of disarray of his lodgings. His bushy grey beard and rough cut hair stood in stark contrast to his alert grey eyes.

"Can I help you?" the recluse offered.

Hayley smiled, trying to put him at ease, "Why, yes. I'm Hayley Chambers, a King's Ranger. Are you Aldus Hearn?"

A pair of teeth revealed themselves as the man smiled, "That's me, though I wonder what brings a King's Ranger to my door."

"I've come seeking some information," she pressed. "Can you help me?"

"Well," he mused, "that depends on what kind of information you're looking for. Why don't you come in and we can discuss it." He walked past her, moving the leather drop aside to enter the hut.

She followed him in, only to be astonished by the state of the hovel. She had been expecting the inside to be as dilapidated as the exterior, but what she saw was a pleasantly normal looking room. He ushered her to the far end, where a small table was set up near the window, the sun streaming through the open shutters.

"Please sit," he invited. "Would you like something to drink? I don't get visitors of the two-legged variety very often."

"Thank you," she responded, "that would be nice." She watched him as he started a fire in the small hearth and then put a kettle to boil, hanging it on a hook over the fire. "I was told in Mattingly, that you're the local expert on wildlife in these parts."

"Well, I'm flattered they think so," he said. "I don't get into town much, my studies keep me busy out here, but I've found the villagers to be friendly enough."

"What is it you study?" she asked. "There doesn't look to be much out here."

"Oh, you're quite wrong, there's much to study here. I've devoted my life to understanding nature and its elemental forces."

"You're an Elementalist?"

"No, not exactly. I prefer the term Animalist, though I suspect you'd be more familiar with the phrase, Earth Mage."

"So you're a mage? You haven't been experimenting with animals have you?" The look of shock on the mage's face told her at once that he hadn't. "Sorry," she apologized, "it's just that some strange creature has been killing livestock."

Aldus Hearn knitted his brows. "Tell me more," he encouraged her.

"I found this at the scene of the latest attack," she said, withdrawing the feather from her tunic and placing it on the table. "Have you seen anything like tit before?"

He picked it up, holding it to the light to see it better. "Fascinating," he muttered, more to himself than anything. "It's quite a good specimen." He ran his fingers across it, and then lifted it to his nose to sniff it. Placing it back on the table, he moved across the room to a cluttered shelf, withdrawing an old book .

"This," he said, "is a book I picked up some years ago." He laid it on the table, careful not to cover the feather. "If I'm not mistaken, this will have the answer."

He began flipping through the pages, and Hayley saw all manner of sketches and notes.

"Are those yours?" she asked.

"This book," he replied, "was handed down to me from my mentor; he got it from his and so on. It's been passed down through the generations. I have added a few observations of my own, of course, but the bulk of the work is not mine. Ah, here it is," he said, at last, stabbing a finger down. "It appears you have found a gryphon!"

"I thought gryphons were only legends," said Hayley.

"Even legends are based on fact. Tell me, what do you know about them?"

"Well," she replied, searching her mind, "they're a cross between two creatures; some say they were created by mages. They have beaks and forelegs like a bird with rear legs like a great cat, don't they?"

"Gryphon's are not some strange abomination. They're creatures that have been around for thousands of years. People try to explain things they don't understand by comparing them to what they know."

"What can you tell me about them? Are they dangerous?"

"The creatures are extremely rare, and it's unusual for them to attack livestock. They normally hunt wild animals, perhaps smaller deer or hares."

"So why would this one be attacking cows?"

"Good question," said Aldus. "Tell me, what's happened recently?"

"I'm afraid I don't understand?"

"What events have transpired in the last few months?" he prompted.

"I'm not from around here," she replied, "so I'm not sure."

"Oh, well, in that case, let me fill you in. Some months ago a group of Norlanders came across the river; it's a common enough occurrence. The local deer have most likely fled, and now the gryphon needs an alternate food source."

"Wouldn't a gryphon just follow the herd?"

"Something must be keeping it here," he said, a smile creeping across his face. "What do you think that might be?"

"Eggs!" she said at last. "It must have a nest. It can't leave its young behind."

"There you see, you've figured it out. Of course, it might be hatchlings, I've no idea how long it takes gryphon eggs to hatch."

"So, I'll have to find its nest. Any idea what type of terrain it likes?"

"It'll no doubt have a cave somewhere, most likely on a cliff face to keep the eggs safe."

"How do I kill it?" she asked.

A look of horror crossed the old man's face, "Kill it? You can't kill it; you'll upset the balance."

Hayley was stunned, "The balance? What are you talking about?"

"This creature is the top of the food chain. It keeps the other predators in check."

"Then what am I supposed to do? I can't let it kill off all the livestock."

"I would suggest you find its lair, and observe it. It'll likely move on once its eggs hatch, and then the cattle will be safe. Besides, if you try to kill it, you'll only make matters worse. An angry gryphon could do frightful damage."

Hayley sat in silence as she thought it through, "I'm still not sure I understand everything. Haven't the raiders been coming for years?"

"On and off, yes, why?"

"So why would the deer flee the area now? Wouldn't they have fled years ago?"

The old man blushed, "I'm afraid that was my fault. I might have warned them to leave. Of course, I didn't realize there was a gryphon in the region."

"You warned them? You mean you can talk to them?"

"More or less, yes," he replied.

"What d'you mean, 'more or less'?"

"Well, I can communicate with them at a rudimentary level. I have much more success talking with the higher level creatures."

"You're full of surprises, Magister," she said.

"Oh please, call me Aldus, I'm not one for titles."

"Anything else you can tell me, Aldus? If I'm going to find this creature, I'll need all the help I can get."

"A creature like this fears little. Chances are it'll fly straight home after making a kill. It'll want fresh meat for its hatchlings."

"I already know the direction it flew off in, so that's good to know."

The old man smiled, "You appear quite resourceful for one so young."

"Thank you," she said. "I am a King's Ranger, after all."

He stood to make the tea, dropping some herbs into the kettle, "So, what's your plan?"

"I'll return to the pasture then head due east into the Artisan Hills. Any idea how far away it might have its lair?"

"I would suspect no more than a day or two overland. It won't want to go too far if it's got a nest on the go. I envy you, you know."

"Why is that," she asked.

"Gryphons are extremely rare; most people live their entire lives without seeing one flying, let alone up close."

"Maybe I'll tame it," she joked. "It would be nice to have one as a steed." The sudden look of dismay on the mage's face made her instantly regret her words, "I'm sorry, I wasn't serious."

"This is no laughing matter," he gently chided, pouring some tea into an earthenware mug. "You can't ride a gryphon, it's not large enough to carry a Human. It's not a dragon, after all."

"A dragon? Are those real too?"

"Of course, though I haven't heard of any around these parts. The ancient tales mention them quite extensively. They've never been common in this land, but across the sea they say the Kurathians have managed to tame them."

"Tame dragons? That would be a sight to see," she said.

"Dragons are known to be highly intelligent. It's said they speak a language akin to the language of magic."

"Magic has a language?"

"Well, we know that the magical runes are universal. It only makes sense that they might support a language, but we're getting off topic."

"Sorry," she offered, "but I love learning about such creatures. What was it you were saying about gryphons?"

"That they're not big enough to carry a Human. Their body is not built for it. Imagine how difficult it would be to run while carrying someone on your shoulders, then imagine trying to fly? It just can't be done."

"Disappointing, but I'll keep that in mind," she responded.

"There have been instances in the distant past when gryphons have befriended mages," he said, "and there's least one story of one coming to a wizard's aid during a fight. Perhaps you'll make a new friend?"

"I can only hope," she said, sipping the tea. "Do they travel in flocks like birds?"

"No, they are solitary creatures. Likely this is due to their size. If they travelled in groups, they'd quickly hunt their prey to extinction."

"You're a wealth of information, Aldus. Thank you," she said.

"You're quite welcome," he replied. "I must say, it's pleasant to have a visitor. The townsfolk never come out this way, though I can hardly blame them."

"Why is that?"

"I think the villagers fear me. I'm the crazy old man who lives deep in the woods. They're more than polite when I come to town, but they likely see me as slightly potty."

"You don't seem crazy to me. What do you do out here, all by yourself?"

"I am a student of nature. I study animals, though I tend to specialize in plant life of various types. I'm fascinated by trees, in particular. What other form of life lives so long and yet is unbent by nature?"

"I have to admit," said Hayley, "I've spent long hours learning about wildlife. I can easily see the temptation. How do you support yourself?"

"I grow food," he said, "or I pick it from the woods. There's much to be found if you know where to look. Perhaps, when this is done, you might come back and visit me. I'd be pleased to teach you a thing or two about plants."

"I'd like that, Aldus," she confessed, "though I fear my ranger duties would prevent a stay of any length."

"Even a short education is better than none," he added. "Feel free to think about it. I'm not going anywhere."

Hayley looked out the window to see the sun casting its afternoon shadows. "I'm afraid I must be off. I need to gather my things. The terrain around here looks rough, and I don't want to take my horse if I have to climb a cliff."

"A good idea," he offered. "I suggest you set off from the village at first light, you've likely got a long way to go."

"I'll keep that in mind. Thank you for your help, Aldus."

"My pleasure, Ranger Hayley," he said.

She quickly downed the rest of her tea and stood, "I'll let you know how things work out."

The old hermit parted the leather hanging for her to leave, "I would appreciate that, thank you."

She made her way back to town, her head full of possibilities. This was going to be the greatest experience of her life!

Three days later Hayley was standing on a hill overlooking a ravine through which a river snaked. It was a precipitous drop, and Hayley was thankful she had left her horse behind. She dropped a small rock over the edge, only to hear it crash into the trees below.

"Doesn't appear to be too far," she said aloud. "Time to find a way down." It wasn't the first cliff she'd climbed, and she was sure it wouldn't be her last. The entire hills needed a new name, she decided, perhaps the Artisan Cliffs would be a suitable label.

The roar of the river grew louder as she descended, her fingers and toes becoming sore from gripping the stone. Finally, she reached the ground and took a moment to shake out her limbs. She was only thirty paces from the water's edge here, with the sound of the running water drowning out all else. Standing at the bank looking upstream, she saw another set of cliffs across the water, but it appeared impossible to climb. Better to cross here, she thought, and try to make her way up top.

She looked down at the water; it was crystal clear here, the rocks plainly visible beneath its surface. She used a stick to steady herself and made her way into the running water. The far bank was only a stone's throw away, but now, with her feet in the cold mountain water, it seemed like an unreachable target. Stepping in, she felt her foot slip on the rocks, forcing her to return to the bank. This was going to be trickier than she had expected.

She considered swimming across but decided the rocks would be just as treacherous, so she moved slightly upstream, hoping for surer footing. Wading in slowly, she took her time with each step, holding her pack above her head to keep it dry. The force of the water was pressing against her, trying to push her further downstream, but she held on, determined to keep her footing. Soon, the water was up to her chest, and she struggled mightily to make progress. The river splashed her face, stealing her breath from her while her limbs became numb.

Almost there, she thought and forced her extremities to work. Thankfully, the water became shallower and then she was out on the other side, shivering despite the warm weather.

She gathered sticks to start a fire and was soon sitting, eating her meagre rations. For three days she had made her way through this inhospitable region only to end up here. "Oh well," she muttered to herself, "I was the one that wanted to be a ranger."

Aldus had gifted her some herbs, and now, as she drank the infused tea, she felt the warmth returning to her limbs. It was quite nice here, away from civilization, and she wondered if anyone had ever been out this way before. She downed the rest of her tea and moved to the river to rinse out her mug.

It was as she was returning to her fire that she noticed the white bones lying at the edge of the forest. She approached, assuming they were the remains of a dead animal. Her theory proved valid as she got close enough to make out a small clearing full of them, all picked clean. This was a bone pile; she must be close indeed.

She doused the fire and packed up her gear, her discomfort all but forgotten. There was a steep hill to her east, leading to the top of the cliffs on this side of the river and she made her way forward, her senses alert. Soon, she was at the top, and the first thing she noticed was the smell; the stench of rotting flesh.

She made her way to the top of the cliff and peered over. Sure enough, below her was a cave opening from which the smell emanated. She listened carefully but heard nothing from below. Dropping her pack to the ground, she began looking for a way down. This, she decided, would be the most dangerous part, for if the creature came home while she was descending the cliff, she would be doomed.

Down she went, one handbreadth at a time. The rock here was exposed, and she found it challenging to grip the stone as she made her way down its face. Finally, she stood looking into the mouth of the cave. The smell was overpowering, and she turned to gulp in fresh air. She closed her eyes, making her way into the entrance, and then opened them, letting them adjust to the darkness.

She thought she saw movement, and then unexpectedly a squawking noise erupted to her left. The cave turned, and as her eyes grew accustomed to the dimness, she made out the forms of three small creatures, in a rough nest of sticks and brambles. The chicks had, no doubt, heard her approach, and, assuming that their mother had returned, bellowed for food. She made her way out of the cave and inhaled some fresh air. Now that she had confirmed the nest, she must make her way back to town. Hopefully, when they realized that the creature would be moving on soon, they would be relieved.

The return to Mattingly was uneventful, and she soon reported to the reeve. The townsfolk were called to the Green Unicorn so that Hayley could give her report. By the time she arrived, the place was packed. Even before she entered, she heard the noise emanating from within. The two entered the building, making their way to a slightly raised area at one end. It was typical for entertainment to use this space, but today it was for this official meeting.

"Quiet down, everybody," Simon yelled, "we have the King's Ranger here to speak with us. She's managed to track down the source of our problems."

"About time!" yelled an angry stocky man.

The talking died down as she put her hands up to get their attention. "I've tracked down the creature responsible for the attacks," she started.

The noise level picked up. "What was it?" demanded a voice.

"A gryphon. Its lair is upriver, on some cliffs."

"Did you kill it?" asked a woman.

"No, it's nesting," she explained.

Simon, who was watching the crowd, turned on her, "What?" he asked, an incredulous look on his face. "What d'ya mean you didn't kill it. That's what we brought you here for."

"There's no need to kill it," she stated. "It'll be moving on as soon as its young can fly."

"Hogswallop," yelled the stout man, "you were brought her to kill that thing! You've failed."

"I was brought here to investigate the problem," Hayley protested, but the crowd's volume intensified. The room was filled with yelling and jeering, but nobody was doing anything until she heard someone call for immediate action.

"We'll go by boat," someone yelled. "There's only one river hereabouts. How hard can it be to find the nest?"

The roar of agreement from the crowd signified the end to the discussion, and then without warning the room was clearing as the villagers stormed out with promises of torches and weapons. She tried to stop them, but they pushed past her, knocking her out of the way in their mad rush out the door.

Somebody grabbed her arm, and she was pulled to the side. She wheeled on them only to see the concerned face of Aldus Hearn peeking out from beneath a hood.

"Come with me," he said, guiding her around the side of the inn.

"That didn't go the way I expected it to," she commented.

"It seldom does," he responded. "The question now is, what you're going to do about it?"

"What can I do? There's no way I can get back there before the townsfolk do. I've led them straight to it!"

"I know a shortcut," the mage said.

"If you knew where it was, why didn't you tell me?"

"I didn't recognize it until you described it. I haven't been there for years, but I know a trail that leads there. Remember, you went due east, over some of the worst terrain imaginable. The animals know an easier trail, though it loops around a bit."

"But they have boats," she pleaded.

"There's rapids that will have to be crossed, that'll slow them down, but you have to move quickly, or it'll be too late. Do you want to stop them, or not?"

Hayley didn't have to think twice. Her father had taught her to do the right thing, regardless of what people thought. "Very well," she said, "I'm in. Tell me how to get there."

She crouched in the bone pile, looking downstream. The boats approached, and she counted at least two dozen people manning them. The men were armed with an assortment of weapons, and even at this range she recognized the look of determination on their faces.

The only way for them to get to the cave was the same route she had taken, so she made her way halfway up the hill, turning to face the oncoming villagers. With her arrows planted in the ground in front of her, she strung her bow. Perhaps, she thought, she could scare them off. She had no desire to kill anyone.

From her position, she was no longer able to see the boats, but the sounds of the hulls grating on the banks of the river announced their arrival. The splashing of boots in water accompanied by the curses of the villagers told her all she needed to know.

Tucked behind a tree, she leaned out to peer around it, watching for their approach. Finally, she spied a group of six men making their way up the hill, their weapons held ready.

"Stop! Don't come any further," she yelled.

There was a cry of alarm, and then a voice called back, "Ranger? Is that you?"

"Leave this area at once," she responded, "in the king's name."

"Bugger the king," a voice responded. "We have to kill that creature."

"I can't let you do that," she replied, her voice steady. "If you don't leave, I'll have to use my bow."

"You wouldn't dare!"

Hayley stepped out enough to get a clear shot. The arrow flew true and struck a tree close to one man's face. The cursing that followed would have turned a Holy Father crimson.

"Saxnor's balls!" bellowed the stout man.

"Leave now, I beg you," pleaded Hayley. "I don't want to hurt anyone."

Things went quiet, and then they all broke their cover at the same time, coming forward in a mad rush. Her two shots put arrows close to their feet, and she watched as they turned tail, and ducked behind cover, cursing yet again.

Time dragged on, and she wondered what the townsfolk were doing, as she heard them shuffling about, but couldn't make out any details. No doubt they were plotting their strategy, and she began to worry. What could she do against all these villagers? The afternoon wore on and then a new problem erupted in her mind. If they waited until darkness, she'd have no way to stop them; her arrows would be next to useless. Would she kill them to make them stop? No, of course not, but she had to somehow convince them that it was her intention.

She was starting to wonder how much time she had left when she heard the second rush begin. At first, there was some crashing sounds from the woods, and then two dozen villagers, armed with spears and pitchforks charged up the hill. She looked on with dismay, hesitating to fire. They were closing the distance quickly when all at once the sturdy man in front crouched down in fear. The others soon followed as Hayley heard a rushing noise behind her. She instinctively ducked, and a large shape flew overhead, no more than an arm's length above her.

It swooped down the hill, weaving its way through the trees with a precision that baffled the mind. Finally, it flew up into the sky and circled. The villagers cowered on the ground, their weapons forgotten. She looked to the sky once more to see the magnificent beast circle the hill, then, with three shapes following it, it headed south, soon disappearing from view. Stunned by what she had witnessed, all she could do was stare south, longing for one more glimpse of the creatures, but soon the reality of her situation became apparent to her as she was surrounded.

"What's the meaning of this," yelled the stout man. "You've no right to do this. You fired on us. We should kill you for that."

"And who would kill a King's Ranger," interrupted a calming voice. The crowd split to reveal a man in hooded robes. He pointed at the leader of the group, "Would you be the one to carry out such a deed? You know it's death to kill a King's Ranger, can you be sure that no one here would reveal that you were the one responsible?"

"Fine," the man grumbled, throwing his club to the ground, "get back to the boats everyone. This is over."

They made their way back to the river bank, leaving the hooded man behind with Hayley. "Well, you seem to have made some new friends," the man said, pulling his hood down to reveal the face of Aldus Hearn.

Hayley smiled, "I don't think I'll be revisiting Mattingly anytime soon."

The old man returned her smile, "They have short memories. Soon, they'll sober up, and be thankful they didn't have to fight the creature. You've done the right thing, Ranger Hayley. Now, I suppose we must make our own way back; I doubt very much they'd be willing to share a boat."

-Interlude IX-

BODDEN

Summer 960 MC

"And that," said Hayley, "was the first, and only time I ever saw a gryphon."

"So far," corrected Albreda.

Hayley looked at the Earth Mage, not sure if she was joking. "Just how, exactly, did you know about that?" she asked.

"Aldus Hearn is a colleague of mine. Besides which, we have a family of gryphon's in the Whitewood."

Baron Fitzwilliam almost spit out his wine, "What?"

Albreda smiled, "Don't worry, Richard, they're a long way from here. The creatures will never trouble Bodden."

"Well, that's a relief," he said, gulping down his drink. "I must say, Albreda, you're full of surprises."

"A fascinating tale, Hayley," said Beverly.

"Yes," agreed Anna, "very interesting. What Aldus Hearn was talking about was real, you know. The great wizard Thromglaster was aided by a gryphon at the battle of Tengart's Trail back in 245."

"Where's that?" asked Gerald. "I don't think I've ever heard of it."

"It's near Redridge," continued Anna, "but that was before Bodden was built. That was the frontier back in those days."

"I think I've heard of it," said Beverly, "wasn't that a Westland invasion."

"Yes, back in the early days of the kingdom. They weren't too happy about Merceria being founded on their doorstep," explained Anna.

"It seems to me," observed the baron, "that we, as a kingdom, spend an inordinate amount of time fighting others."

"Well," said Hayley, "Merceria was founded by mercenaries. I suppose warfare has been in our blood for generations."

"Yes," agreed Anna, "but we need to make peace with our enemies, they're people just like us."

"Agreed," added Gerald.

Baron Fitzwilliam chuckled, "An interesting observation, Gerald, considering your background."

"What do you mean, Father?" asked Beverly.

"It wasn't all that long ago that a young Gerald Matheson would have wanted to kill all the Norlanders."

Anna looked to her friend, "Is that true, Gerald? You always told me that they were people, just like us."

Gerald blushed, "It's true, Anna. After the death of my family, I sought only revenge."

Anna rose, making her way over, and took his hand tenderly in her own, "I'm sorry for your loss, Gerald. I know how hard it was for you. Tell me, what changed your mind about them?"

Gerald took a deep breath, letting it out slowly, "It was just after I was made Sergeant-at-Arms. It all started when I fell into the river…"

Gerald and the Norlander: Part I

Spring 934 MC

There was a crispness to the cool spring air that nearly took Gerald's breath away as he rode. This past winter had been harsh, but now the warmth of the spring, cold as it was, threatened to melt the snow with great speed, turning the ground to mush.

Beside him rode Blackwood, while the rest of the patrol followed behind them in pairs. He spotted the strange twisted elm tree that marked the boundaries of the Ramstead farm and the outer limit of today's patrol. Pushing his horse into a faster trot, he looked forward to soon returning to the warmth of the Keep. He was about to say as much to Blackwood when something caught his attention. He listened intently, trying to place the sound, and there it was again; the familiar noise of fighting.

He drew his sword, urging his horse into a gallop, the rest of his patrol automatically picking up speed in response to his actions. There was a thicket of trees, and the moment he rounded them, he was brought back to his earliest memories with the dreadful scene that awaited him.

Just like his own father years ago, an older man lay strewn on the ground, his blood staining the earth crimson, while a woman bent over him, weeping inconsolably. Nearby, a Norlander hacked at a young lad, who deftly ducked behind a well and crouched for safety. Gerald roared as he drew his sword, and the raider attacking the youth looked up to see vengeance charging down upon him. The enemy called out in alarm and then ran for cover.

Half a dozen men erupted from the house, one dragging a young girl by the forearm. As arrows began to fly, Gerald felt one hit his armour, but the mail held and it deflected harmlessly off him. He ignored the archers, charging at the man dragging the girl. His sword slashed across the back of the bastard's head, collapsing the raider to the ground, releasing the girl from his clutches.

Swordplay erupted all around him as the patrol joined in the fray. He twisted in the saddle, spotted another raider running for his horse, and then turned his mount to charge the man, cutting into his lower back even as the raider attempted to leap into the saddle. These men were vermin, Gerald thought, and deserved no pity!

He heard horses and wheeled about, trying to get his bearings. To the north he saw half a dozen riders who had managed to get on their mounts and were fleeing, riding hard for the river that formed the border of their two lands. Norland horses were smaller than the Mercerian mounts, but their riders wore less armour. They would quickly outdistance the patrol from Bodden. He spat on the ground in disgust.

Leaving Blackwood and four men to help the farmers look after the dead, Gerald and the remaining men pursued the raiders. There was not much chance that they would catch them, but he must follow, lest they turn back to do more damage.

Clearing the edge of the farm, he spied them in the distance, trotting along, secure in the knowledge of their escape. His frustration turned to elation when he watched them turn eastward, and he realized his chance. There was only one ford around here, and it lay north of the wood, but the enemy, unfamiliar with this area, rode east, to circumnavigate the forest. Gerald, knowing the pathways here, made his decision, and plunged into the woods, his men close behind. With any luck, he would arrive at the river just before the enemy.

The forest was thick, and the going was slower than he had hoped for. The ground was wet, and the horses slipped through the mud as they pushed forward. He was forced to slow the pace and cursed at his bad luck. Finally, emerging from the woods, Gerald looked down at river before him. The raiding party had fled the farm at the first sign of the Bodden patrol, giving them a head start, but now they struggled to cross the river, for the spring thaw had raised the level of the water. The enemy had to pick their way carefully across the ford, lest they fall into the raging waters.

Gerald urged the patrol forward, and they charged downhill toward the disorganized Norlanders, his men yelling their triumph. They had brought their enemy to heel, and now the invaders would pay the price. The horses' hooves thundered toward the river, their excitement mounting the closer they got. All day long Gerald's men had raced through the forest to beat the enemy here, and now the raiders were trapped.

The patrol rushed into the swirling river, eager to come to grips with the enemy, and was soon up to their flanks in the swiftly running water. Gerald struck out with his sword, feeling the tip penetrate an opponent's leather jerkin. As he pulled it back, blood gushed down his blade. The rider toppled from his saddle and was carried away by the fast flowing water.

Gerald received a blow on his shield and turned his head back to observe the tip of a spear glancing off of it. The Norlander holding it, pulled it back for another thrust, so Gerald stood in his stirrups and reached out with his own blade, striking overhand to bring it crashing down on his enemy's head. The weapon penetrated his foe's helmet, cutting deeply. Gerald tried to pull his sword free, but it was stuck, and he twisted his wrist in an effort to loosen it. Stretched out as he was, there was nothing he could do to block a blow from another opponent, who rose in his saddle for the killing blow. Gerald ducked low and to the left, releasing his grip on his sword. The manoeuvre threw all his weight to the left side of his saddle and this, combined with the force of the water coming from his right, sent his horse tumbling into the river.

Luckily, he had instinctively pulled his feet from his stirrups to avoid being crushed by his mount, and then a wall of water slammed into him, sending him spinning. In the blink of an eye, he was beneath the surface, fighting for breath against the coldness of the water. All thoughts of the fight were torn from his mind as he struggled to gain control of his momentum. His armour pulled him down, and he felt the rocks of the riverbed scraping against him as the current forced him downstream.

He released his shield to free his arm; then tried to grip anything to stop his whirling. His hand grasped a branch of some type, and he struggled to hold on, pulling himself upward. He finally broke the surface and took a breath, only to find his numb hands unable to hold their lifeline. He gulped air while he could, before the cold water pulled him down once more. Struggling to hold his breath, he tried to take stock of his predicament. It would be nearly impossible to remove his mail while being tossed about the river in this manner. He must endeavour to reach the nearest bank to pull himself from the river's icy grip.

His numb hands reached out, but he couldn't feel anything around him. With lungs burning from the lack of air, he was just about to pass out when he bounced off a boulder in the river, thrusting his head above the surface once more. He gasped for what air he could as the river carried him through a set of rapids. The turbulence here made it difficult for him to breath, with as much water as air entering his lungs. The swirling maelstrom tossed him around like a rag doll. His ribs struck a rock, and then his legs bounced from one obstacle to another, each one leaving its mark upon him.

With his energy ebbing fast, he was driven sideways into a large rock, and he clung to it for all he was worth. He lifted his head above the water, seeing the shoreline only a few horse's lengths away. Struggling to pull himself upright, he scanned the shore, trying to find the best way to safety. Just downriver there was an ancient tree, with an expansive root system that jutted out into the water. If he could throw himself close enough, the current should take him where he wanted to go.

With a deep breath, he hurled himself towards the northern bank. The icy water tried, instead, to pull him into a final embrace as his armour snagged on a branch. Desperately, he reached out, barely managing to grasp a root before the water closed over him one last time. He hung on by sheer willpower, his legs dangling uselessly beneath him with no riverbed to stand on. Using every ounce of energy at his disposal, he dragged himself, hand over hand, toward the bank.

Gerald crawled onto the dirt and collapsed, his lungs burning with the effort. Coughing up water, he was dismayed to see blood; he had taken a beating. First, he must find someplace to rest, if only for a little while. Lifting himself up, he glanced around, coming to the realization that he was on the wrong side of the river; this was Norland territory.

Over the rushing of the water, he thought he heard something, footsteps perhaps? He must find cover, Norland soldiers might be looking for him. He spied a fallen tree trunk a stone's throw away and dragged himself toward it. It reminded him of all those years ago when he had fled the men that killed his family. Then, he was a frightened boy, but today, he was a hardened warrior, able to defend himself. He had lost his sword, but his dagger was still sheathed on his belt. He drew it, seeing the sun glint off it as he held it in front of him. He may be injured, he thought, but he would go down fighting.

Peering over the trunk, he watched a Norlander emerge from the brush. There was a pole across his shoulders, with a bucket hanging over either end. He had the look of someone down on his luck with his unkempt hair, rough looking beard and threadbare clothes. The man stopped by the river, lowering the buckets to the ground. He was apparently going to fill each container, but as he stooped to grab the first bucket, he spied Gerald's drag marks emerging from the water. His eyes began to follow the trail, and Gerald cursed; now he would have to expend what little remaining energy he had to silence the man before he raised the alarm.

Leaving the buckets by the riverbank, the stranger began moving toward Gerald's position; soon he would be clearly visible. Gerald struggled to rise, the pain in his ribs reminding him of the rock he had bounced off.

"I mean you no harm," the stranger said.

"You're a Norlander," Gerald spat, wincing as he spoke, his dagger shaking in front of him from his exertions.

"And you're evidently a Mercerian, but you're still someone in need. I won't hold the sins of your forefathers against you."

Gerald struggled to grasp the man's meaning. A spasm of pain wracked his body and he instinctively dropped the blade, clutching his ribs. "Get away from me you filthy Norlander!" he barked.

"I can help you," the man countered. "You're injured."

"I'd rather die than accept help from northern scum."

"So be it, friend. I wish you well, it's likely to be a cold one tonight." The stranger gathered his buckets, filling them from the river and then, hoisting them back onto his yoke, carried them away.

Gerald listened to the water sloshing as he left and then finally relaxed. He tried to piece together the time and came to the conclusion it was late afternoon. He wasn't hungry, and there was plenty of water, but he was shivering and must find warmth or he would freeze to death.

He briefly considered swimming the river for it would be better if he was on the Mercerian side, but reasoned against it. The river had tried to take his life once, he would not tempt fate a second time. He knew he should remove his armour for it held the cold, but he was afraid that enemy soldiers might show up at any time. He thought of fire and made his decision; he would gather some wood and attempt to light it. He tried to rise to his feet, but the pain in his ribs robbed him of the act, and he sat back down in agony.

"For Saxnor's sake," he muttered, "I hope you've a better fate in store for me than freezing to death."

He thought back to the days of his youth and remembered spending a night under a trunk. It worked then, and it just might work now, he reasoned. He used his dagger to start digging beneath the old tree trunk. It was tough work, but finally, as it darkness descended, he had cleared enough space to crawl beneath to give him a semblance of protection.

The work had warmed him, and he pulled himself into his protective cover, but soon he regretted his decision. His present lack of movement meant the chilly air began penetrating his limbs, leaving him shivering uncontrollably. He thought to divest himself of his armour, but his hands were too numb, and he cursed the weather.

Darkness soon came, and with it even more frigid temperatures. Gerald didn't know how long he lay there, shaking with the cold, but he could no longer feel his arms or legs. He passed into delirium; saw himself wandering through the fields of his youth. He was shaken awake by a pair of hands; the Norlander had returned.

"Let's get you somewhere safe, shall we," the stranger suggested, "before the patrols find you."

"Patrols?" stammered Gerald, barely able to talk.

"Yes, they're always looking for Mercerians crossing the border. We need to get you to safety. I have a small farm nearby, but it'll take some time to get there in your condition. Can you walk?"

Gerald grunted a curse, but the words wouldn't form between his chattering teeth.

"Come then, let's get you away from here," the man came closer, and Gerald accepted his assistance. His rescuer placed his arm around his shoulder, and soon the two hobbled away from the river.

Gerald opened his eyes to a small room. He was lying on a simple cot, with a rolled up blanket beneath his head. He remembered little of his trip to arrive here, but his entire body ached. Turning his head, he peered about; the room was sparsely furnished and quite run down. There was a table with two chairs that looked like they might soon fall apart. Across the room, was a simple window bracketed with a pair of shutters that appeared warped from many years of use.

The smell of food greeted his nostrils, and he rotated his view to see a fireplace against the far wall, a small pot hanging over it. His host, stooped over the food, was ladling something into a small wooden bowl. The stranger turned, his eyebrows going up as their eyes met.

"Ah," he said, "I see you're awake. I thought you might like some food. I've a nice root stew for you here."

Gerald sat up, wincing with the effort and spat, "I'll not take help from a Norlander."

"I'm afraid you already have, my friend," the man replied.

Gerald tried to rise, but as he dropped his feet over the edge of the bed, he doubled over in pain.

"Take it easy," his host advised, "you've damaged some ribs. It's likely to be a few days before you can move around. Here try this, it's not much, but it'll help."

A bowl of food was offered, but Gerald pushed it aside. "I don't want your help," he growled.

The man placed the bowl down, putting his hands into the air, "So be it. I'm Kaylan Rothmire, and this is my home, humble as it is. Might it be too much to ask who you are?"

"Your enemy," Gerald replied with venom.

"And yet I've never laid eyes on you. Why is it that you have so much hatred toward Norlanders?"

"You know why!" said Gerald, through gritted teeth.

"I am but a simple farmer," Kaylan responded.

"You're no farmer," snarled Gerald.

"I assure you I am, but let us not argue. I have some chores to attend to. I'll leave the bowl of food here on the table for you. It's entirely up to you if you want to avail yourself of it." He exited the building, closing the wooden door behind him.

Gerald looked around the room, searching for any chance of escape. He tried to rise again, but the pain was too severe, and he sat back down, defeated. The room gave no clue as to his captor's identity, but he knew he was no farmer; the man was too well-spoken, and yet here he was, in this run-down hovel. He lay back down, trying to ease the pain of his ribs. Perhaps after more rest, he might be able to move around a little more. Mere moments later, he was fast asleep.

He awoke sometime later to the sound of chopping wood. It seemed like early morning, and he realized with a start, that he must have slept the night away. His head felt clear, and so he rose, experimentally, to a sitting position. His ribs ached, and he moved slowly to avoid more pain.

Rising to his feet, his head swam, and so he steadied himself with one hand on the wall as he made his way to the table, where the bowl still lay. He noticed a plain white apron hanging beside the hearth. Was there a woman here? He wandered over to the fireplace to glance into the pot; it was empty. Had the man given him the last of his food; it seemed unlikely, Norlanders were not known for their hospitality.

Gerald struggled back to the cot; he was still weak from the battering he had taken, and he knew he had no choice but to rest. Laying his head down, he felt the weariness envelope him once again and closed his eyes.

The sound of a door opening jarred Gerald from his slumber. He noticed

Kaylan carrying in some wood that he dropped by the fireplace. "Feeling better?" the man asked.

"Why, what's it to you?" Gerald replied. "Does it matter? You're only going to kill me anyway."

Kaylan turned, surprised by the venom in his voice, "Do you think I would go to the trouble of saving you if I was only going to kill you? That hardly seems worth the trouble."

"I suppose not," admitted Gerald. "Still, you're a Norlander, and I'm a Mercerian."

"We're not so different, you and I. I suspect you've suffered a great loss, as have I." The man's forlorn look was lost on Gerald, who merely grunted.

"Did you say your name was Kaylan?" Gerald asked at last.

"Yes, Kaylan Rothmire."

The room fell into silence while Gerald tried to make sense of his situation. He was at home on the battlefield, but here, in enemy territory, he was out of his depth.

"Are you hungry?" asked his host.

"No, I'm fine," Gerald lied. "Where's my dagger?"

Kaylan rose to his feet, walking over to the hearth, "It's right here, above the fireplace. It's yours whenever you want it. I have to go back outside for a while, there's food to be gathered."

"I thought you were a farmer?" Gerald queried.

"I am, but it's the spring, and I haven't enough stores left from winter. I need to go into the woods nearby and gather some plants, or we'll both starve. Unless, of course, that's your intention?"

"No," Gerald reluctantly agreed. "Be about your business Norlander, I'll not interfere."

"Very well then," said Kaylan. "I should be back before dark. Feel free to make yourself at home."

Once more his captor left, and Gerald began to wonder at the man's sanity. Gerald's dagger lay only a few feet from him and yet he hadn't moved to hide it. What was his host playing at? He struggled to his feet and made his way to the fireplace, steadying his progress by placing his hands against the wall. The dagger was where Kaylan had left it, and Gerald tucked it into his belt, and then staggered back to his bed. He struggled to think of a way to escape, considering his options before finally making a decision; he would kill his captor and then make his way home.

-Interlude X-

BODDEN

Summer 960 MC

"I just don't see you killing a man who rescued you," offered Beverly.

"I was different in those days," replied Gerald. "I was a man possessed. The loss I'd suffered destroyed me."

"It's true, Beverly," added the baron. "You didn't know the old Gerald. He had lost his humanity somewhere along the line. All he did was train or fight."

"But you're not that way now," commented Anna.

"I remember you from the archery contest, you didn't seem like that," offered Hayley.

"That was years later," explained Gerald.

"How old are you, exactly?" asked Hayley.

"Gerald's ancient," said Anna, "but we still love him, don't we Tempus!"

The great dog barked his agreement as everyone laughed.

"I can look back on it now and see my behaviour was wrong," said Gerald, "but at the time, all I could think about was vengeance."

"Still," offered the baron, "without that fire burning in you, you wouldn't have become the warrior you are today. Even the bad times in our lives shape us in ways we can seldom see, at least at the time."

"Wise words, Richard," offered Albreda, who was now sitting on the floor beside the baron's chair. "You have the makings of a sage."

Fitz smiled at his companion, "I've learned from the best."

"Please continue, Gerald," said Beverly. "It's a fascinating story. I knew you lost your family, but I never knew about this."

"Of course, Lady Beverly," Gerald mused. "Where was I?"

"You were about to slaughter the Norlander in his sleep," supplied Anna.

"Really?" said Gerald. "I don't remember using the word 'slaughter.'"

"Well, you didn't use that precise word, but the meaning was clear."

"I suppose that was the meaning, at the time," he offered. "I was waiting for him to return so I could 'slaughter' him, to use the princess's precise term…"

Gerald and the Norlander: Part II

Spring 934 MC

It was dark by the time Kaylan returned. Gerald lay on the bed, pretending to be sleeping as listened intently to his host. It didn't take long for the man to climb into his own bed and fall asleep. Gerald counted to five hundred in his head, and then sat up, carefully swinging his legs over the edge of the bed. Grasping the dagger firmly in his right hand, he stood, wincing with the effort. Taking a few steps toward his host, he steadied his movement by holding onto the nearby chair. He staggered, scraping the chair along the floor, and froze, fearful that his captor might awaken. Letting his breath out slowly, he regained his composure and continued his journey. Soon, he stood over Kaylan with the dagger in his hand. He placed it at the man's throat, ready to cut, but his hand shook, and he couldn't do it.

"Go ahead," said Kaylan, his eyes opening suddenly. "Do us both a favour and take me out of my misery."

Gerald, unexpectedly overcome with a flood of emotions, withdrew the blade, tossing it across the room. He staggered back, his legs collapsing beneath him as he crumpled to the floor. He could feel tears forming in his eyes and fought to control his breathing.

Kaylan was now standing over him, a worried look on his face, "What is it? Tell me."

"I can't do it," he said. "I promised to kill every Norlander I encountered, but I just can't do it," he sobbed out loud. The past washed over him in a flood of emotions, "The murderers killed my little girl! All I can see at night is her face, staring up at me. I've failed them!"

Kaylan put a hand on his shoulder, "Be at peace, friend, for you are not the only one to suffer. I, too, lost a family to the wars."

Gerald stared back at him. "I don't understand," he said.

"I wasn't always a farmer you know; I used to be a soldier."

Gerald was immediately on edge, "A soldier?"

"No longer, my friend, you can relax." Kaylan watched as Gerald took a breath. "I gave up that life to settle down, raise a family."

Gerald glanced at the apron on the wall. "Your wife's?" he asked.

Kaylan turned his gaze, "It's all I have left of her now. We had a son, but he's lost to me."

"I'm sorry," said Gerald, feeling for the man. "I know what it's like to lose your loved ones."

Kaylan's face turned bitter, "My son didn't die. He took service with the earl, against my wishes. There are only two careers for the common man in this part of the country, farmer or warrior. He was lured by the false promise of riches. All they have to do, they're told, is take it from the Mercerians, but it's not true, only death lies south of the river."

Gerald wasn't sure how to respond, "I would have said the same of Norland, I suppose. We've been fighting each other for generations."

"Tell me," prompted Kaylan, "does the average Mercerian farmer worry about such things?"

"No," he responded, "farmers only worry about whether the crops will come in, they care little for politics."

"It's the same here, my friend. Now rest, sleep easy, you'll be safe enough while you heal. A few weeks and you'll be able to return home."

Several days later Gerald was comfortable enough to walk around the tiny house without using support. His ribs still ached, but a herbal tea brewed by Kaylan helped offset the pain. He was eager to be on his way but knew he wouldn't get far in the condition he was in. He sat at the table while his host stoked the fire.

"Did you say your name was Rothmire?"

"Yes," said Kaylan. "What of it?"

"It sounds Mercerian," stated Gerald.

His host looked startled, "Hardly surprising really, when you think of the history we share."

"What d'you mean?" asked Gerald.

"You see, we all come from the same stock." Kaylan watched him, and evidently saw the look of confusion that crossed his face. "You don't know about our shared history, do you?"

"No," Gerald admitted.

"Norland was founded by Mercerians who were fleeing the tyranny of the king. Of course, that was generations ago."

"Fleeing tyranny?" Despite, or maybe because of his hatred of Norlanders, Gerald was intrigued.

"That's what the nobles are always claiming. They trace their heritage straight back to the royal line of Merceria."

"So you're saying the King of Norland claims the throne?"

"Well, not the present king. It's actually the Earl of Beaconsgate who claims an unbroken bloodline to your throne. He's obsessed with reclaiming it."

If this was true, Gerald thought, it certainly explained the attacks on Bodden. "And how do you feel about all this?" he asked.

"I don't care for politics, I've seen too much of the effects of it. All I want to do now is live in peace. If Norlanders reach across into your lands, you're more than welcome to kill them, but it's not the commoner's fault. We're all victims here. The troops steal as much from us as from you."

"What d'you mean?" asked Gerald.

"The earl wants his men to support themselves. They help themselves to food and drink on both sides of the river."

"Surely the earl protects his tenants?"

"Hah!" exclaimed Kaylan. "The earl could care less. All he cares about is taking back Merceria, and his share of any loot, of course. As you no doubt have noticed, I have little here in the way of belongings."

"I should like to help in some way," offered Gerald. "What can I do?"

"For now, nothing. You'd only make your condition worse. Rest as best as you can, and in another week you'll be ready to do more."

The sound of horses in the distance drew Kaylan's attention, "I suspect we're about to have visitors. I suggest you come with me."

"Where are we going?" Gerald asked.

"I have a small cellar; there's an entrance beside the house. I'm afraid you'll have to hide behind some barrels. If they find you here, it won't go down well for either of us."

Gerald rose, following his host. At the side of the house was, as he had indicated, a small hatch, leading into a tiny room stacked with crates and barrels. "Wouldn't you get a reward for turning me in?" he asked.

"No, they don't give rewards. They'd likely just kill the both of us. You must be silent, regardless of what you hear." He ushered Gerald into the small, cramped cellar, closing the door, and securing the latch, effectively locking his guest in.

Gerald remained hidden in the darkened room, listening intently, straining to make out the conversation.

"And to what do I owe the pleasure of this visit?" Kaylan asked.

"We've come on the orders of the earl," a man said in a high pitch. "We need supplies."

"I have nothing to give," defied Kaylan.

"We'll see that for ourselves, old man," said the same voice. Gerald heard the man as he dropped from the saddle, his armour clattering as he walked. The sound was drawing nearer, and he feared the visitor might be coming to the cellar. He squeezed in behind some barrels, crouching as low as he could. Sure enough, the cellar door opened and there was a man, silhouetted by light.

"You seem to have plenty down here," the visitor was saying. "Let's see what's available."

Footsteps descended, and the visitor was so close Gerald could almost hear him breathing. A sword pried open a barrel, and he peered inside. "These are empty!" he swore.

"As I said," argued Kaylan, "I have nothing left to give. You lot have taken anything of value."

The visitor tapped each crate and barrel with the hilt of his sword, only to be rewarded with the echo of empty containers. He grumbled and then withdrew, his footfalls disappearing up the steps.

"I'll report this to my captain," the high pitched man said, "but he won't be happy. I suspect he'll want to come back himself."

"Whatever you feel is best," replied Kaylan, in a neutral tone. Armour jingled while the man remounted his horse and then Gerald listened as the horse's hooves receded in the distance. A moment later, Kaylan called down the steps, "It's safe to come out now."

"What was that all about?" Gerald asked.

"The army is short of supplies, as normal. The soldiers do this all the time. There's nothing left for them to take, but it doesn't stop them from trying."

"I had no idea it was this bad," Gerald confessed. "The Baron of Bodden would never condone such activities."

"Would that the baron ruled here," commiserated Kaylan, "perhaps we'd all be better off."

As time passed, Gerald's bruises healed, but his ribs were still tender. Kaylan planted seeds in the small plot he called his farm, while Gerald helped by tending to a small herb garden to the side of the house. The work was simple enough and didn't require him to overexert himself. Kaylan had proved to be a gracious host. Though he had little to offer, he was always willing to share. Gerald felt guilty being such a burden on the man and resolved to leave him some coins when he left.

The weather had become warmer, and Gerald could tell that summer was just around the corner. He moved around now without discomfort but still, occasionally, a twinge of pain would cause him to double over. It was over a month since their last visitors, and he was taking a breather on a small stool, in front of the house. Kaylan was chopping wood near the edge of the clearing, and the rhythmic sound of the axe lulled Gerald into a drowsy state.

A shout of alarm brought Gerald back from his near-slumber, and he looked up to see Kaylan pointing off in the distance where three horsemen were cresting the rise. The farmer ran back to the hut, shouting at Gerald, "You must hide in the root cellar, quickly!"

Gerald did as he was bidden, once again crouching behind the barrels. The cellar door closed, the latch falling into place and he waited, straining his ears to pick up any sign of what was transpiring. The hoof beats drew closer, and then he heard the horses halting very near to the hut.

Kaylan's voice quite clearly stated, "I suppose this isn't a social call?"

"Where is it?" said a well-spoken voice, full of contempt. "I know you've got it hidden around here somewhere."

"I have nothing left, you've seen to that. You've taken everything of value from me."

"It seems I don't quite have everything, old man" the visitor sneered. "Hand it over."

"You'll never have it," said Kaylan. "You're not worthy of it."

"Why are you being so obstinate, old man? You know it's rightfully mine. Give it to me!"

"You'll never get it, Joseph," Kaylan spat. "I'll take its location to the grave with me."

"So be it," the younger man said with finality.

The sound of rasping steel was all that Gerald heard before Kaylan screamed out in pain. Then, the visitor yelled and cursed as he rained down blows on the poor farmer, his screams echoing through the small cellar. Gerald ran to the door to push it open, but the latch held and all he could do was listen as his friend was attacked. The screaming finally stopped, the air now filled with only the sound of the heavy beating of his own heart.

"Search the place; leave no stone unturned. It has to be here somewhere!"

Gerald backed up, drawing his dagger. He stood in the darkest corner of the cellar and waited, knowing their eyes would have to adjust to the gloom. There was a rattling noise as the latch was withdrawn, and then the cellar door swung open, casting a dim light into the small space.

Two men peered down into the gloom. Gerald watched them intently, but they didn't enter.

"I searched this last time," one of them uttered, "no sense in looking again." They turned, closing the cellar door behind them.

Gerald listened to them ransacking the house, but could hear no sound of Kaylan. With nothing but a dagger against their armour and swords, he could do little but wait, not knowing his friend's fate. Eventually, the sounds stopped, and he heard voices from above.

"It's not here, sir."

"Damn him to the Underworld," their leader cursed. "It must be here somewhere."

"We are due back in camp by dark, sir."

"Yes. We'll have to come back another time."

"What about the farmer?"

"Leave him. He can die where he lies."

Gerald emerged from the cellar, after waiting what seemed like an eternity for the riders to leave. It took a moment for his eyes to adjust to the sunlight. The soldiers were disappearing over the rise as he cast about, searching for Kaylan. He spied him on the ground, close to the front of the house. A large pool of blood spread beneath his inert form, though his chest was still rising and falling. Gerald ran to help him, but one sight of the terrible stomach wound told him all he needed to know. He knelt beside the injured man.

"Kaylan," he said, "is there anything I can do?"

"I'm afraid it's the end for me," his host replied. "I don't have much time. Will you grant me a final wish?"

"Of course," said Gerald, tears forming, "name it."

"Beneath the garden where you worked, is buried an old heirloom. Take it and put it to use. May it serve you well."

"I can't..." stammered Gerald.

"Please," Kaylan begged, "I cannot bear to see it in the hands of someone who would use it for evil."

"That man," asked Gerald, "was he your son?"

"No longer," rasped Kaylan. "He deserves nothing but a dishonourable death. I would die in peace if I knew I went after him."

"Then I will kill him," promised Gerald. "I shall track him down to the ends of the earth if need be, but I must see to you first."

"No, you must act quickly. Your presence here will not delay my trip to the Afterlife, though I suspect I go to the Underworld for my actions."

"I can't believe that," objected Gerald. "You have treated me with kindness and respect, something I didn't expect from a Norlander. You have taught me that we are all the same, regardless of what side of the river we're from."

"Then I die without reservations," uttered Kaylan with his final breath, "knowing that I have made a friend of a Mercerian." His eyes closed, his chest rising no more.

Gerald looked down upon him, seeing, not a Norlander, but a companion; a friend. "I will avenge your death," he proclaimed, "of that, you may be sure."

He left Kaylan's body where it was and took up a shovel. Digging into the herb garden with abandon, he was rewarded with the sight of burlap. He knelt, unearthing the buried treasure with his bare hands. By the size and shape, it was a weapon of some sort. He tore away the wrappings, freeing a sword that was of an old design, with a small crossguard that was popular generations ago. The blade was well made, its hilt decorated with gold and gems. He lifted it in his hands, surprised by its lightness. Looking to the sky, he saw the sun was just passed its peak; still some time left before darkness would lose him the trail. Gerald entered the house, likely for the last time he thought, and retrieved his battered mail. Now was the time for retribution; to make good on his oath to Kaylan.

The sun set as Captain Joseph Rothmire finished another goblet of wine. "A fine blend, Stilson," he pronounced, smacking his lips.

"I'm glad you approve, sir," the sergeant replied. "I've some more if you like? Got it from that farm we raided last week."

The captain smiled, "I knew I kept you around for a reason."

"Bit disappointing today, sir," mused Stilson.

"He wasn't going to give it up," cursed the Captain. "I should have known. He probably sold it years ago."

"Pity," added the sergeant, "from the sounds of it, it would be quite valuable."

"Oh, it is," the captain agreed, "but I won't waste any more time on it. Next week we'll cross the border again. No doubt the Mercerian farmers will yield more food than our own."

"It'll be good to be rid of this area," muttered the sergeant.

"Why is that?"

"Don't you know? They call this place the Warrior's Rest."

"I've never heard that. Tell me more," commanded the captain.

"They say the ghosts of fallen warriors reside here, sir. Best to be away as quickly as possible."

"Nonsense," announced his superior. "Now I've got to go and piss out this wine. I'll be back shortly." He staggered out of the tent, steadying himself carefully on the ropes as he exited. He took a moment to catch his bearings, and then wobbled toward the tree-line, his mind still flooded with visions of the ancient sword. He walked up to a tree and, placing a hand on its trunk to steady himself, fumbled with his trousers before dropping them to his ankles. Looking down as he sought his relief, he saw a blade suddenly protrude from his chest. In the blink of an eye, he was dead, falling to the ground to lie in his own piss, still steaming from the chill of the air.

Sergeant Stilson fished around in his pack, withdrawing another bottle. Sitting back down to pour more wine, he heard the tent flap open behind him and spoke, "It's about time you got back. I thought we might celebrate the coming invasion."

The silence behind him had him turning to see what was the matter. At the entrance to the tent was an ancient spirit, wearing old and tattered chainmail, grasping a bejewelled blade, still dripping with blood. The sergeant's face grew pale, and his hands began to tremble, for surely this was a warrior spirit that stood before him.

"Begone from this place," it said, "and never return or join the fate of your captain."

The sergeant tried to stammer out a reply, but his voice froze in fear.

The ghost before him spoke again, "I have no wish to take your life, for I have seen enough death this day. Go, and never let me lay eyes upon on you again!"

The sergeant flew out the tent, pausing only long enough to call on his men to flee.

Gerald sat down at the small folding table. He had expected a long fight, but somehow Saxnor had protected him, and his enemies now flew in abject fear. He didn't know why, but the weariness of the past few hours wore heavily on him, and he merely acknowledged his good fortune.

Gerald stood for a moment, gazing down into the Kaylan's grave. His friend had told him to take the sword, but instead, he laid it on the body, so that the dead man could take it with him to the Afterlife. Saxnor would see his strength and welcome him with open arms. He deserved no less.

He finished filling in the grave and then stood, resting his arms on the shovel, looking down. "Goodbye, my friend," he said aloud. "May you find eternal happiness in the Afterlife."

He lit the house on fire, to announce to Saxnor that a worthy warrior was coming, and then strode away south, toward the river and home.

-Interlude XI-

BODDEN

Summer 960 MC

The room was quiet for some time. Gerald sipped at his ale; there was a feeling of gloom hanging over the room.

"It is the burden of the commoners to bear the brunt of war, I'm afraid," said the baron at last. "I wish it were not so."

"I had no idea the Norlanders claimed the Mercerian throne," said Hayley.

"Oh yes," offered Anna. "It all dates back to the year 520."

"Why, what happened in 520?" asked Beverly.

Anna smiled, pleased that her knowledge would once again prove useful this evening, "In that year the King of Merceria was King Talran. He had two sons, Talburn and Talrith. Talburn disagreed with his father's rule and tried to take the throne for himself."

"Why would he do that?" asked Beverly. "All he had to do was wait till his father died."

"I don't know why, but he raised an army and marched on Kingsford, that was the capital back then. He was defeated at the Battle of the Hills, and fled north with the remainder of his followers."

"Why didn't they track him down?" asked Hayley.

"They tried, but the crown had taken heavy losses in the battle. Talburn managed to get away, and we now know he made it to Norland. His brother Talrith became king in his place when their father finally died."

"It's called the sundering," offered the baron. "It's not something they like to talk about in the capital these days."

"I can see why" offered Anna. "It wouldn't look good to have someone survive an attempt to take the throne."

"The Norlanders have been trouble ever since," offered Albreda. "Though anyone outside of the border region wouldn't know it. They've harassed the Whitewood for generations."

"Well," interrupted the baron, "I suppose we should bring this little get together to an end. It's getting late, and we all have things to do tomorrow."

"Just one more tale?" requested Anna.

"We've all told a story," Gerald reminded the princess.

"Then I'll tell one," said Anna, a determined look on her face.

"Very well, Your Highness," said Fitz, "feel free to share your tale."

"Well," she started, "it's the story of Tempus. He was a mighty warrior dog who grew up in Merceria."

Albreda rose, moving over the large beast, gently laying her hands on his forehead. He looked up at her, his tail wagging slightly. "I don't think he grew up in Merceria," she commented.

"What do you mean? Of course, he grew up in Merceria, I've known him for years."

"Yes, but he was full grown when you met him," Albreda reminded her.

"Wait," said Anna, "are you saying you can talk to him?"

"Well, I wouldn't say talk exactly, but yes, I can communicate with him." Anna was enthralled, "What does he say?"

Albreda smiled, "I think it's quite evident that he loves you very much."

Anna beamed, "And I love him too, you can tell him that."

"Oh, he knows that already. Do you want to know how he came to be your dog?"

"Yes," she replied, "I mean, I know the king sent him to Uxley, but I don't know much more than that."

"I'm afraid it isn't the nicest of stories, are you sure you want to hear?"

"Yes," Anna said, solemnly, "now I need to know the truth."

"Very well," said Albreda, "I will reveal his story, though you must remember it is seen through the eyes of a dog."

"How does it begin?" asked Anna.

"Much like Gerald's tale," offered Albreda. "With water…"

A Dog's Tale: Part I

Year Unknown

"Our tale starts at sea," began Albreda, "though I cannot fathom how long ago it was. There was a great storm that struck a ship, near the shores of Westland."

The ship shuddered as the great wave crashed against the hull. The Captain, long used to sea travel, tried to brush it off, but the look in his eyes told his crew this was a storm of the Gods. Onward the ship ploughed, rising on the crest of one wave only to fall into the deep valley formed by the trough. The bow drove down, biting deep into the water while the next wave swamped over the deck, sending men scrambling for safety. Another great heave of the ocean carried the wooden vessel soaring up, but as it plummeted down again, the ship gave out a mighty groan as the hull began to split.

Beneath the deck water sluiced upon the kennels that held mighty Kurathian Mastiffs, bred for war, each capable of tearing the legs from under a galloping horse. It was an expensive cargo; these creatures had been bred for generations to be the epitome of the fighting dog.

In one kennel, a tiny pup tried to stand, but the rocking ship skittered the young hound across the floor to bang up against the bars of his cage. It let out a yelp, and its mother, out of concern, sniffed the air. There was a loud cracking noise, then the planks of the hull split, and water starting pouring in. Yelling and screaming could be heard above the roar of the storm, and the young pup saw Humans scuttling past. The water level began to rise, and then the ship lurched as if striking some great beast. Everything pitched violently forward and the cages, held in place with rope, collapsed, their metal frames bending as they piled in on each other.

The pup, in wild-eyed panic, pushed itself through the bent bars, desperate to escape the water. It turned to see its mother lying lifeless within. Pawing at the bars, it would have stayed till the end, but someone, in their bid to escape the hold, opened the upper hatch and a flood of water rushed in, carrying the tiny dog toward the back of the ship.

As the water rose, the creature paddled as best it could, desperate to keep its head above water. There was a mighty crash, and suddenly the ship disintegrated. He was thrown into the maelstrom, swirled around by the currents, and he struggled to swim through waves that tossed him about wildly. He watched the ship sink, seeing its masts disappearing below the waves like felled trees.

A tremendous swell broke, thundering down on him, driving him deep into the water where his descent to the depths was only stopped when he struck sand. The current scraped him onward, throwing him ashore upon a sandy beach. Bits of debris came hurtling along after him as the God's fury dragged the remnants of the ship from the sea. He struggled to survive the lashing of the wind and rain, crawling under cover of whatever he could find. Finally, beneath the debris, he cowered, until, at last, sleep came.

"Miriam, don't go far!" the man yelled. Off to the south, he watched his young daughter running across the sand. It had been a terrible storm, and now they combed the beach, looking for anything useful the sea might have washed ashore. At the very least, some driftwood would prove helpful. The farm was always in need of firewood, and gathering driftwood was far less work than cutting down trees.

There was a lot of debris, and he couldn't help but feel sorry for whatever ship had been destroyed. There were deck planks and tarred ropes in abundance, along with barrels and such. With any luck, they might find a lantern or two that he could resell in the city.

"It's a ship, Papa," the young girl proclaimed excitedly. "I bet it's got treasure!"

"Careful now," he called out, "I don't want you getting hurt. There's bound to be sharp edges and splinters."

The young girl poked her way through the wreckage with a stick. "There's cloth over here," she yelled, "come have a look."

The man made his way over in anticipation. This was luck indeed, for a ship's sailcloth would prove most useful. There was a larger section of debris, with the sail, tattered and torn as it was, draping over it. The father started pulling out timbers of a manageable size while his daughter poked around some more with her stick.

"It's moving," she called, "come quick."

He dropped the beam he was trying to shift to run over to her. Half expecting the wind to be playing tricks, he was surprised to see movement beneath the linen sail.

"Stand back," he warned. "It's probably just a crab or something, but we must be careful." He took the stick from her, using its tip to gently lift the edge of the sail. There was movement beneath, something with light brown hair, definitely not a crab! He put the stick under the material, using both hands to flip up the sailcloth.

"It's a puppy," the girl yelled. "Oh, look, do you think it's hurt?"

The father had been searching the beach all his life, but never had he seen such a sight. He crouched down near the tiny dog, placing his hand upon it. "He's still breathing," he said. "The poor creature must have been on the ship. Come on, let's take him home with us."

The little girl smiled, "Is he ours now, Papa?"

Her father smiled back, "Malin himself has seen fit to have him survive last night's tempest and bring him to us. Yes, I believe he is meant to be ours."

"Tempus?"

"No, tempest. It's a big storm, you understand?"

"Yes, Papa. A Tempus is a very big storm."

The man chuckled, "Very well, what do you think we should call this creature?"

"Tempus," she declared.

"You mean Tempest?"

"Yes," she repeated, "Tempus."

He cradled the poor creature as they made their way back to the farm.

"Life was good for young Tempus," continued Albreda, "for he had a loving family. He was well fed and guarded the farm for them, but sadly, all good things must come to an end."

Tempus lay on the floor as feet shuffled past. Today the house was quiet, despite the number of people present. They talked in hushed tones and the little girl, her face wet with tears, was taken into her father's room. She emerged, moments later, her face buried in her mother's dress.

Later in the morning, they brought the father out. He was laid in a wooden box; its top sealed. The sound of the hammer, driving the nails into the wood sounded ominous, as if warning the Afterlife that someone was coming.

Tempus watched, saddened by the look on the face of the little girl who had loved her father so deeply. Her mother, robed in black, followed the procession as it left the house, the little girl following meekly, her hand held in that of her mother. The beast stirred, rising to his feet, no longer the tiny puppy of a time gone by. He was tall now, his head resting at the level of most people's waists. He turned his wrinkled countenance to watch as the visitors filed out the door into the field beyond. Following along behind them, he heard wailing and turned to see a man in blue robes raising his hands above his head, with a staff in one hand. From his throat issued forth the clear notes of a song and soon the others joined in, the harmonies melding to form a lament.

Tempus howled, the sound blending with the soulful tones of the others. Soon, the hymn finished, and they gathered around a hole where the father, within his box, was gently lowered into the ground. More words were said, and then a single voice rang out as the little girl serenaded her father with one last song.

The crowd dispersed, saying their farewells while three men began to fill in the hole. He trotted over, sniffing the ground as they dug; this was the smell of death. His name was called, and he turned to see the little girl, beckoning him. No longer would he hear his master call his name, no longer would the father be there to look after his little girl. I must guard her now, he thought, it is what he would have wanted.

Sometime later he sat watching as the last of the belongings were put into a wagon. The farm had proven too much for the mother, and she was taking her daughter away from this place. He leaped into the back of the wagon and soon the rhythmic steps of the horse commenced. He watched as the house that had been his home disappeared into the distance while they trundled down the road.

For most of his short life, he had lived on the farm, remembering little of his experiences before. The future was unknown, but as they travelled the road, he caught a whiff of new scents, heard new sounds and thought he was on a great adventure.

Later in the day the smells changed, no longer did the fresh air of the country cross his nose, now he detected a foul odour as if the land was covered in excrement. The road turned bumpy, and soon the horse's hooves clattered loudly as their feet struck a hard surface. It was jarring, the change, and Tempus looked over the back of the wagon to see small stones, tightly fitted together. He looked up to see towering structures, much larger than the farm that had been his home for so long.

The wagon stopped, and the mother climbed down from the cart, helped by the fellow in charge of the horses. She knocked on a door, and soon a rough looking man with an unkempt beard appeared. Coins changed hands, and the man placed a key into her palm. She walked down two more entranceways and unlocked the door; this was to be their new home.

Tempus dropped to the ground and trotted over while the driver started unloading the wagon. The mother had called over the little girl, and they stepped inside, their faithful dog behind them. The smell of the place caused him to wrinkle his nose; the stench of the city permeated it. The walls were filthy, the rooms empty, with a threadbare cloth hanging limply in the only window, its shutters twisted and warped.

The mother turned to the child, and he watched her weep openly. Was this their future now?

They had only been in their new home for a couple of days when the trouble began. The rough looking man appeared at the door, a wooden stick in his hand. There was an argument, and he struck the woman, forcing his way in. Tempus rose from his place, but the woman bid him stay. He watched, confused, as the intruder berated her, felt her hair, then placed his face close to hers, all the while talking in threatening tones. Tempus growled at the wretch, who turned, pointed the stick at him, yelling, before finally leaving their home.

From then on, whenever the rough man visited, Tempus would be ordered to sit in the kitchen with the child, while grunts and shrieks erupted from the mother's room. Each time he would return to see her sitting, shattered, crouched in the corner holding her knees to her chest. Soon, the scoundrel began spending more time at the home. He would push the woman out the door in the mornings, and later, after it was dark, she would return, worn out and ragged, to deposit coins in his hands. Tempus hated the man, and his hackles would rise when he smelled the gin-soaked fiend approaching.

It finally came to a head one day. The woman had been pushed out the door, and the young girl was dressing while Tempus lay on the floor. The door flung open, and the brute stepped through the doorway to leer at the girl. He grabbed her roughly by the arm, and she screamed. Tempus sprang into action, leaping on him. Surprised by the sudden burst of speed, the man let go, tumbling to the floor, and then the huge dog was upon him, clamping his teeth down on the man's forearm; how dare he threaten his mistress!

Blood spurted from the man's arm, and he yelled out in pain. He kicked Tempus, but the great beast easily absorbed the blows. Down bit his powerful jaws and Tempus felt bones crushing between his teeth. There was a thud to the side of his head, and he released his grip. The man had grabbed a chair with his other hand and brought it crashing down on his opponent. The scoundrel scrambled to the door, his blood leaving a slimy trail upon the floor. Tempus leaped after him, but he was too slow as the door closed on him. He sat, listening to the man dragging himself away, calling for help. Fearful for his mistress' safety, he turned to see her shrunken into the corner, her eyes wild with fear. He tried to calm her, but the closer he got to her, the more fearful she looked.

He turned back to the doorway, determined to guard her with his life. It didn't take long for retribution to come. There was yelling outside, and then a group of men entered the house. The door to the girl's room opened and half a dozen men stood ready with sticks and spears, the injured man safely behind them. In they came and the fight was on.

Tempus lunged out, sinking his teeth into a calf, the man screaming in agony, and then a flurry of blows descended on the dog as the room flooded with men. They looped a rope around his neck, and then pulled him from his feet, binding his legs. Despite his struggles, he was soon subdued, unable to move as they dragged him from the room. Someone grabbed his mistress. He heard her screams, and then the rough man held her tightly by the upper arm. A different man with long stringy hair stooped to look down at Tempus, nodding as he sized the beast up. He stood, depositing some coins in the rough man's hands, and then the group of them dragged the dog out of the house.

Outside there was a small, two-wheeled cart with a cage on the back. Four men lifted him up, locking him in the cage and then they began to move down the street. Tempus, helpless in his bondage, could only look on in despair as the house disappeared from view while the distant screams of his mistress echoed behind him.

They rode down the narrow, cobbled streets, the uneven stones rocking the cart as it made its way through the stench. There was blood here, smelled Tempus, blood and death. The wagon halted, and then men came and dragged him from his cage through a large open door of a two-storey wooden building. Inside, he saw many crates and barrels as he was pulled along, the smell of saltwater fresh in the air. He heard the sound of water somewhere; the gentle sloshing of tiny waves upon stone.

They hauled him past a sunken pit in a cleared space near the middle of the building. Around this were seats, empty at this moment. Daylight leaked in through some shutters near the roof, reminding Tempus of the ship from so long ago, yet this structure was larger and didn't move.

He was finally pushed into a cage of sturdy metal construction, secured by a latch on the door. Someone reached through the bars and cut the ropes binding his legs. He tried to get to his feet, but he was weak and lay still, merely observing those around him. He heard breathing nearby, and then all at once, the room erupted in a cacophony of barks and howls that filled the chamber. For the first time in his life, Tempus was truly afraid.

Over the next few days, he was beaten and starved. Men were continually waking him by poking him with sticks, and he grew irritated. The sounds of dogs fighting, snarls and yaps, carried easily through the large room. Every evening people entered, and he watched them take up their seats around the pit. This was it, his punishment for failing to protect his mistress would be to die here.

Finally, one evening they came to his cage, and it was his turn. They had poles with a loop of rope around one end, and they used these to hook the loops around his neck. It took four men to guide him to the pit, with Tempus fighting all the way. He was led down a ramp, and then they opened a gate, revealing the sandy floor of the fighting ring itself. They released the ropes and bolted for the gate, narrowly missing his teeth as he turned on them. He slammed up against the metal gate, but it held, and he backed up in a fury, growling menacingly. A similar growl erupted behind him, and he turned to see a large dog with coarse fur, comparable to him in height. Seeing the wild look in the creature's eyes, Tempus guessed what was about to happen.

His opponent lunged forward, eliciting a roar from the crowd. Tempus met his rival head-on, with the two mighty beasts striking mid-air, crashing to the ground in a flurry of teeth and claws. Over and over the two rolled, the coarse-haired dog nipping at his flanks. Tempus was the larger of the two but lacked the dexterity to reach throat of his adversary. His opponent, more nimble, rolled under his defense to bite into Tempus' exposed throat, but the mighty mastiff's thick skin and wrinkled neck saved him. With blood pouring from his wounds, he shook his whole body, loosening his enemy's grip. Tempus then rolled out of the way, releasing himself from the jaws, coming to his feet instantly, ready to counter-attack.

They stood facing each other for a moment, blood pooling by Tempus' front paws. His opponent, unharmed, charged toward him. Tempus bent his head low, and,as his enemy rushed to strike, he turned his head and opened his mouth wide, launching himself forward. He grabbed the creature by the throat and began crushing it with his jaws. His opponent struggled, but even at this young age, Tempus had the weight on him. Down came his jaws until there was a crunching feeling and the dog went limp.

Cheers erupted from the crowd, intermingled with the distinctive sound of coins passing hands. Something had changed, he thought; things change when coins are heard. He was led back to his cage. He lacked the energy to resist this time. There, waiting for him, to his amazement, was food. So this was how it was now? So be it.

"I cannot tell," said Albreda, "how long this continued, but it became a way of life for him. I suspect it might have been a year or more. The crowds grew bigger, more coins changed hands, and Tempus grew. Soon, he filled the building with people as they came to see the mighty pit fighter, but his fame caught up with him. Eventually, there was no dog to fight him, and that's when things changed, again."

Tempus strutted from his cage. The name of the game was survival; he did what was necessary to live. Perhaps one day he would find his family again, to rescue his mistress from her torment, but for now, he must survive. For countless battles he had endured, often fighting two opponents at once. He had grown considerably, and he now stood with his head level to a man's chest. His body had widened; he was now a full grown Kurathian Mastiff, and though he didn't know it, he was the size of a small pony. His battles became less frequent as it became harder and harder to find suitable opponents for him.

He was the main attraction that packed the arena, making his owners a large purse each fight. He was paraded in front of the crowd to gasps and applause, and when he fought, the building shook with the reverberation of their cheers.

It was a typical evening; the sun having set, the crowd warmed up with other dogs fighting each other. Soon, they would come for him, he knew, and then, when the fight was over, he could eat. Food was ever in his mind, for a creature of his size needed a lot of it to survive, and his captors never seemed to give him enough, leaving him longing for more. The gate opened as the noose passed over his neck. It was a ritual now, nothing more. He had tried to escape the rope in the past, but the result had only been pain. Now he submitted meekly, saving his frustration for the pit.

They led him to the arena, the crowd rising to their feet in applause as he entered. The noise deafened him, and he glanced about, as he usually did, to judge the watchers. His eyes took in a stranger in a blue jacket, so out of place among the earthy tones worn by the others. The man watched Tempus intensely, his hand on his chin, stroking a thinly cropped beard.

A low growl distracted him from the crowd, and he turned to look at his opponent, expecting to see a large dog or two. What met his gaze was far more distressing than a group of dogs, however, for opposite him, held in place by a chain, was a mighty creature, the likes of which he had never seen before. It was fully twice the mass of a Human, with coarse brown fur and long dark claws. It stood on its rear legs with its forelegs in the air and, as he watched, it opened its mouth to issue forth a roar that shook the very air.

The beast was held in place by a chain that looped through a ring in the floor and then was passed through to someone in the stands. Now they let go of the metal tether, and the creature dropped to its four legs and surged forward. Tempus attacked the same way he always did, bending his head low, coming up at the last moment to sink his jaws into his enemy's throat. This time, however, as he prepared to lunge, a sharp pain erupted in his side when the creature slashed out, sending him sprawling, blood gushing from his wounds. He staggered to his feet and ran, narrowly escaping another swing of the terrifying claws. The creature seemed to be everywhere. Tempus ducked and swayed in a frantic effort to avoid the beast's attempts to slice him open.

The crowd was yelling, but something else was happening, suddenly the people began booing, and Tempus didn't understand. He backed up against the wall of the pit and was struck from behind by a sharp stick. He turned in anger, and one of the handlers backed up. It was a mistake, for with his attention diverted, the powerful creature sank its teeth into his flank. Pain erupted, and Tempus rolled in a desperate attempt to get away. His foe released its hold, and he struck out, snapping at the beast's leg. He felt his teeth catch on the coarse fur and then he bit again, thrusting his head forward for further purchase. Down went his jaw, straining to penetrate the thick skin of the beast.

It let out a roar of pain and then rained down blow after blow on his back, trying to free its legs. The razor-sharp claws opened up his hide, his lifeblood pouring out of him. In desperation, he clamped down harder, and his jaws did their work, crunching through bone, until they met, and then he released. His opponent fell backwards, unable to remain standing, a cry of agony echoing through the room.

The crowd went wild, their yelling and screaming drowning out all else. Tempus, weak from blood loss, waited and as the creature raised its head in pain, he struck, throwing all his mass into a desperate attempt to reach the mighty beast's throat. He hit his target, toppling the creature over, but it struck out violently as Tempus gained the upper hand. Once again, he forced his jaws to close till the effort almost killed him. Finally, the struggling stopped, and he released, rolling off the body. There was a wild eruption of applause, and then he collapsed, too weak to even lift his head.

He lay in his cage, unable to move without his wounds searing in excruciating pain. They came and poked and prodded him, but he no longer cared. He was too far gone to find his mistress now; all his fighting had been for naught. He didn't even raise his head to eat, so they stopped bringing food. Initially, they had slathered his wounds with some grease, but after two days, they ceased doing even that.

He was waiting for the final release of death when he saw the man in the blue-jacket again, looking through the cage at him, talking. He heard his name and saw the man holding his old collar, the name Tempus carved into it by the little girl. How long ago that seemed. He wondered what had happened to her; perhaps he would see her in the Afterlife?

The blue-jacketed man stood up, withdrawing a small bag from his belt. Coins changed hands again, and Tempus wondered what this portended. He soon found out for they loaded him into the back of another wagon, along with an assortment of other dogs. He lay quietly, watching the city disappear into the background as they made their way north, the smell of the sea carried away by the wind.

For weeks they travelled while he lay in the cage, near death. In the evenings the man fed him by hand, pouring a liquid down his throat, and slowly he began to heal. By the time they arrived at their destination, he was sitting up again and had resumed eating solid food. He was a mass of scars and cuts, and while moving pained him, at least he was still alive. The wagon entered the streets of a new city; there was a different smell here.

They were near water, but not the salt water he was used to. Lo and behold, the wagon rounded a corner, and he saw a river to one side, its wide channel carrying water south.

The wagon halted, and a man came out of a building. He spoke, and Tempus realized the man was of the same breed that manned the ship so long ago. He wore a kerchief around his neck and had the smell of dogs about him. The cage was opened, and he snapped a collar around Tempus' neck. The kerchiefed man looked at the old one, now worn with age and combat. "Tempus," the man said, nodding. He stared into Tempus' eyes with a look of understanding and rapped out orders.

Tempus was led into a building. It was open, much like the last, but this time there were no crates or barrels, but brick built kennels, each with its own door. They were open-topped, with walls too high to jump. The masters here could look down on the animals, but at least there was room to stretch. Tempus entered his new home and lay in the straw provided. A bowl of water sat nearby, and he settled in and fell asleep.

A few days later he was visited by his new masters. The blue-jacketed man spoke to the man with the kerchief, who was holding something in his hand. The first man nodded, and his companion entered the kennel, producing a collar. It had spikes on it, and he held it up in front of Tempus' face. There was a metal plate on it with writing, but its significance was lost on him. The man tightened it around his neck and pat him on the head. Where things about to get better? He doubted it.

With his strength recovered, they soon began exercising him, running him through obstacles. The kerchiefed man, who seemed foreign to this place, appeared to know all about him. He stretched him to the limit of his abilities. He was taught to jump higher, run faster and respond to commands. When Tempus ignored him, he would be struck by a whip, and he soon learned it was easier to submit, for there was no escape from this place, just like the last.

They began pitting him against other dogs, but there was no crowd, and he was never permitted to kill them. He learned to respond immediately to commands and won rewards; food and rest.

Eventually, the day came, as he knew it would, to once again take his place before the crowds. He was led into a large building, with an open roof. Benches lined the sides of the oval structure, and at one end was a group of men and women in fine clothes, raised above the rest of the crowd. He was trotted out by the kerchiefed man who made a pronouncement. Words were exchanged with a man in the fancy box, and then he was trotted back to the far end of the arena. Soon, three other men appeared at the far end, each with a hound on a leash. The men all looked at the box, and then a red flag was dropped. The leads were released, and with a howl, all three dogs ran straight for Tempus.

Tempus felt the leash release him, but a word of command held him in check. His handler backed up, climbing to a seat nearby, out of harm, and Tempus waited.

The three dogs elongated their gait, one out-pacing the others. Tempus waited, ready to spring at a moment's notice. The lead dog drew closer, and he saw the animal was exhausting himself in his mad dash. Finally, his release command was given, and he launched his own attack. There was the briefest of moments where the crowd watched him as he leaped, and then he dug his teeth into the first attacker. Twisting his head, he ripped his opponent's throat open and then swirled to face the remaining two. He growled at one to his left and started for it when he heard a sharp whistle from his handler. He turned suddenly to his right and struck low, grabbing his enemy's paw in his mouth. The hounds were fast but slight, and his bite ripped the skin open. The creature yelped, and Tempus released, turning back to his last opponent.

He lowered his head for the impending charge. As his last adversary leaped, Tempus went even lower, the creature sailing over his head, snapping as he went. He rotated to face his opponent and struck quickly, digging his teeth into the soft flesh of his flank as he turned. He heard the command and released, allowing his opponent to slink away. The fight was over, the crowd was applauding, and Tempus was once again, a champion.

-Interlude XII-

BODDEN

Summer 960 MC

"It was a rough life, full of death and pain, but he did what he needed to survive," Albreda tried to explain.

"It sounds horrible," said Anna, stroking her dog's back. "He didn't have any friends, no one to care for him."

"It's a barbaric practice, fighting dogs," stated the baron. "If it were up to me I'd banish it."

"Still, you can't fault Tempus for fighting," said Beverly. "It's what he was trained to do."

"I can't help but feel some unease," revealed Hayley, "to think we're so close to a creature that has caused so much death."

"Really?" admonished Albreda. "Do you feel uncomfortable sitting near Sergeant Matheson here, or the baron?"

"No, why?"

"They've both killed scores of men. Does their presence make you feel uncomfortable?"

"No," the ranger admitted, "I suppose not."

"It's a valid point," said Anna, nuzzling Tempus. "Tempus wouldn't hurt anyone here, would you, boy?"

As if in answer the great dog let out a large yawn and stretched his legs.

"So most of his life was spent in Westland?" queried Anna. "How did he come to Merceria?"

"We shall see," said Albreda. "Now you must remember I'm seeing images and feeling emotions, so it's all subject to my interpretation."

"Still," said Gerald, "it's a fascinating tale. I feel a strange sense of camaraderie with him."

"You've always felt that way," Anna reminded him. "You and Tempus are very similar in a lot of ways."

The baron smiled for he could easily see the similarity. "Still, we should get back to the story before the morning light comes streaming through the shutters."

Beverly sat up, "Is it truly that late?"

"No, my dear," said Albreda, "your father's exaggerating, but it is getting late."

"Then I pray you continue, good Albreda," said Anna with a great flourish, "for I'm thrilled to hear the tale of the heroic mastiff."

"Very well," the mage capitulated. "Now, where were we…"

A Dog's Tale: Part II

Year Unknown

"Fighting had become his whole existence by this time. I can't tell precisely how much time had passed, but he was full grown, and I believe several years may have come and gone."

Tempus was hauled out of his cage in the pre-dawn. He knew what this meant; training, as the fighting ring was quiet in the early hours of the day. They led him to the edge of the arena and another dog, a wolfhound of some type, was dragged into the fighting pit. Tempus growled and stood ready, but much to his surprise, instead of being commanded to attack, he was walked towards the other dog, still on his leash.

The two animals growled and barked, but the handlers held them, applied sticks and issued commands. This continued for some time until both beasts grew quiet. Tempus was taken back to his kennel, and the other dog was kennelled beside him. What were they up to?

Over the next several days this process was repeated until they would enter the arena without snarling or growling. The next part of their training involved placing them in the ring without their leashes. They growled and circled each other, but the 'do not attack' command was whistled, and both contestants instantly obeyed.

Tempus grew accustomed to the great wolfhound, and soon, they would stand side by side in the arena with little more than a sniff of each other. An evening came when their bond was tested. The crowds were particularly noisy this eve when Tempus and the wolfhound made their way into the arena. Standing at one end while the crowd's applause died down, they waited, unsure of what to expect.

At the far end of the arena, the gate opened, revealing four strange looking dogs. They had coarse fur, long legs and their bushy tails remained low as they entered. Tempus had never seen such animals before and observed how they moved swiftly in a coordinated manner. They hunted as a pack, and he suspected they had fought this way before. He heard the wolfhound let out a howl and shifted to stand closer. This would be close-in work, and they needed to protect each other's back, or they would be torn to pieces.

With a growl, the enemies slowly advanced. They did not bark, but snarled as they walked, spreading out in a line, trying to flank them. Tempus listened for the commands, the whistles that told him what to do, but none came. Soon, the two comrades were surrounded; the wolfhound facing one way, while Tempus guarded the other.

The pack attacked in a rush, darting in, one at a time to nip at the defender's flanks. The strikes were quick, and Tempus found no time to do anything other than react. The enemy repeated this several times, and Tempus came to the realization that the pack was testing their defence. The great mastiff had fought many times and had learned his lessons well. He timed their movements and waited. The largest of the creatures made his run, and then Tempus shifted, correctly predicting the next one's advance. He lunged to his right, catching his opponent off guard and sank his teeth into its neck. He maintained his grip while the smaller beast thrashed and suddenly another was on his back. He felt sharp teeth bury themselves deeply, but held on, determined to wreak as much damage as possible.

He heard a growl, and then the wolfhound pounced, pulling the creature from Tempus' back. Tempus let go of his target as the remaining two surged forward. There was a whirlwind of fur and gnashing teeth. He could briefly see his first target slinking away, blood pouring from its wound, but soon more teeth sank into him as something bit into his leg. He yelped in pain, desperately turning to meet his new attacker, but the creature let go, retreating with blood dripping from its mouth.

A yelp erupted beside him, and he turned to see the wolfhound on the ground, two dogs upon him. Tempus ignored the pain in his leg, and propelled himself forward, barrelling into one, knocking him from his partner's body, his teeth digging deep. He clenched his jaws trying to find the bone, but the tuft of fur on his opponent was thick, and he struggled while more teeth nipped at his legs, but he knew he must hold on until he heard the familiar snap. On and on came the enemy and soon, Tempus was covered in his own blood. His thick skin saved him, for their teeth, though sharp, could not fully penetrate his hide. Covered in surface wounds, he bit down even harder and finally felt the neck snap, his opponent going limp. He pulled his muzzle away from the carcass to turn on those that remained. The wolfhound had a death grip on another's leg, the creature bleeding out while two others circled, occasionally rushing forward to bite him.

Tempus found the energy to move, willing himself to continue the fight. The other creatures were distracted trying to take down the wolfhound, and so he waited. Soon, the pack went in again, and as they began to withdraw, he struck, using his paws to push one down, then using his bulk to pin it to the ground. His teeth found purchase and dug into the creature's throat; its thrashing lasting only a moment before it too, went still.

The wolfhound, now finished with its first victim, turned and the last animal must have known it was doomed. The two dogs circled their prey before it made one final, hopeless charge. It was all over in an instant as the two great pit fighters finished off their victim. The crowd erupted in applause, and the handlers came to take them away after their triumph.

Dozens of times over the coming months they worked together, though they still fought independently from time to time. The crowds seemed to love their partnership, but it became difficult to find suitable opponents. They usually battled other dogs, but one match they also defeated a bear and then a wild cat of some type. Each time they worked as a team they learned each other's tactics better and began to count on each other's cooperation.

It was a night like many others; the crowds could clearly be heard from the kennels. He listened as the early fights were carried out. Smaller dogs would start, chasing rats around, with coins changing hands at the conclusion. Then came the slightly larger dogs, snarling and growling. The sounds were all too familiar to Tempus; they had become his way of life. He knew he would fight last, the champion of the pits to finish off the evening. What would they have him fight tonight, he wondered?

Before long, it was his time, and he strode confidently into the ring, alone. So, it was to be a solo fight this evening! He waited patiently for the opposite gate to open, wondering what his adversary might be. The gates soon swung out to reveal his opponent, the great wolfhound. Tempus was confused, who were they to fight and why hadn't they come out the same door?

They both trotted to the centre of the ring, taking up a position back to back, each staring at an entrance. The crowd booed, and Tempus didn't understand; where were their opponents. He heard the command 'attack' but could see no target. The noise of the crowd intensified, and soon men came from the kennels with spears in their hands. Tempus was used to these tools, for their points were sharp. Were they to fight men this evening?

The handlers gathered around, yelling at Tempus and the wolfhound. They poked and prodded, repeated the 'attack' commands, but neither of them took action. There was more yelling, and soon the kerchiefed man showed up. Leashes were attached, and both animals were escorted from the ring as people threw all manner of garbage into the arena. Tempus had never seen its like before. What were they doing?

Both were taken back to the kennels, but this time they were put into cages, facing one another. Men stood to either side, spears ready, with points facing each animal.

The kerchiefed man looked at Tempus, then at the wolfhound, yelling so much that spittle erupted from his mouth. He chopped his right hand down onto his left and then suddenly there was a yelp as two spears drove into the wolfhound's flanks. Tempus looked on in horror as his friend, impaled, let out a dying whimper. Tempus readied himself; so this was it, he thought. If I am to die tonight, I shall take as many with me as I can.

He snarled and moved back and forth as best he could in the cage. The spears stood ready but didn't move. How dare they taunt him like this, he thought, am I not the champion? Let them kill me now for I shall never fight for them again. He was removed from the cage and taken back to his kennel, struggling the whole way. The kerchiefed man came to visit him but merely shook his head.

Days went by, and he grew hungry and thirsty, but no food was forthcoming. When they finally came to take him to practice, he laid down and refused to move. Tempus was determined to avenge the death of his only friend by refusing to ever fight again.

Ready to die, he lay quietly in his cell, waiting for the inevitable, but once again fate intervened. He lay on his side, his eyes closed, hunger gripping his belly when he heard voices. He glanced at the door to his cell to see a well-dressed man. He sported a bushy grey beard and knelt at the kennel's gate. Tempus met his gaze, and the man held out something, reaching through the bars.

Tempus, his inquisitive nature taking over, rose unsteadily to his feet, moving toward the well-dressed man. He stopped short, smelling the air; there was food here. He stepped forward, taking the proffered treat. It was a small wafer, but immensely filling. Was it magic? He felt a hand upon his forehead. He wanted to attack, to rend his victim for all the injustices he had faced, but feeling some tenderness in the touch, he just remained still, too weak to care anymore.

The well-dressed man withdrew his hand, then stood and turned to face the kerchiefed man. Tempus heard coins changing hands and knew his life was to change once again.

That evening he was fed a proper meal, and his handlers spared him the usual taunts. The next morning they brought a cage on wheels, and led him into it, chaining his collar to the base. Soon, the wagon was trundling out of his home, and he squinted as the sunlight struck him directly for the first time in years.

As they rolled through the town he marvelled at the sights. He stared at the people walking on the streets, and one little girl stopped to watch as he rolled by. He thought, at first, it was his mistress, but her hair was the wrong colour. He slumped back down, looking back on his life. Why had he been born, he wondered, why must he be so tormented. Was the maker mad at him?

He smelled water, and the wagon halted. Soon, they pulled him from his cage, leading him up a long ramp to a large wooden boat. He stood on its deck, and he was reminded of the place he was born, but here the water was calm and didn't smell of salt. They took him below, and he was chained once more.

Sometime later the gentle rocking of the boat told him it was in motion. He knew not where it was going, only that the sound of coins had once again changed his destiny.

"He arrived in Kingsford," explained Albreda. *"I can see it before me as clear as day. I suspect his story is nearing its close, though there is still much to tell."*

In this new city, there was a grand building, made of stone, and Tempus was taken there as soon as he left the boat. The well-dressed man led him, with handlers behind holding the Tempus' leash. The air here seemed fresher, for there was a breeze, though perhaps it just seemed sweeter after the close confines of the lower deck. They halted, outside of an immense structure and brought chains to secure him. So, he thought, they want whoever's inside to be kept safe from me. They led him in, and he meekly followed, determined to see this through to the end.

The great room they were taken into reminded Tempus of the warehouse, but this was made of stone and much more grandiose. Instead of barrels and crates, he saw strange stone figures and suits of metal on stands. Men with spears stood on either side of the room as he was led toward a man robed in red, seated in a large chair that rose above him, glittering with gold.

He heard the word 'Majesty', and everyone in the group bowed. The man in the seat rose and walked forward. Tempus felt the chains grow tighter but watched patiently. The man was pale of skin but had dark, black hair with a neatly trimmed beard. Tempus waited as the stranger in the red-robe walked around him, nodding to the well-dressed man. Returning to his seat, he spoke, and someone scuttled forth to drop coins into the well-dressed man's hands. Once again, fate had intervened.

Life serving the man in the seat turned out to be little different from his past. He was fed more and kept in nicer kennels, but still, he fought other dogs. Each time the man in the seat would watch over him, collecting coins every match.

The fights grew less frequent, but he was still undefeated, and he wondered where the endless stream of opponents came from. He seldom killed his adversaries these days, merely maimed them and he was surprised to see the same opponent after a severe mauling. He mulled over this for some time, but eventually gave up; there were some things he just could not explain.

The weather turned cooler, and he was packed into a wagon for travel. For many days he journeyed until they entered a great walled city.

"Tempus had arrived in Wincaster," added Albreda, "for I know the city well. I can see it clearly in his mind for this is almost the end of his story. He would still fight in the capital, but there were few dogs large enough to provide a challenge for him. He had likely made the king a tidy sum, for he was impossible to defeat."

Tempus rose from his bed, his limbs aching. Years in the pits had left him scarred and his body devastated. His joints pained him, and his teeth were chipped. His constant fighting over the years had taken its toll.

They came for him, like any other night, securing the chain to his collar.

Off they marched him, but instead of entering the ring, they led him from the building to a wagon. Here he was caged, and the horses trotted off, lumbering up the street. Tempus was confused, was there some new development? Where was the sound of coins?

The wagon stopped, and he was removed from his cage. Led by a loose leash, he trotted on, feeling every step shake his bones. Into a magnificent structure he marched, his handlers besides him. He looked left and right, wondering where he would fight next.

There was a great hall, similar to where he first met the seated man, and into this he was led. There, once again, his benefactor looked down on him, a smile upon his lips. The man rose, and Tempus felt the chains tightening as his handlers took precautions. Two men in metal stepped up with spear tips pointed at him. He knew what was coming, for this would be the end.

The man leaned forward, staring Tempus directly in the face. Their eyes met, and Tempus let out a slight whimper. He wanted to go out in a fight, but he was broken and tired. Please, he thought, put an end to my misery. The man placed his hand upon Tempus' head, feeling his scarred fur. He stepped back, calling someone to his side. A smaller, bald man came forward with something, and Tempus saw a new collar. In place of the spikes, this one had a single brass plate with something on it. Was it a magic ward to protect him?

The guards raised their spears as the bald man stepped forward timidly, fighting to remove the old collar. Soon, the new replaced the old, and the chains were removed. Tempus looked about, surprised and astounded. The seated man held out his hand, and someone put a leash in it. He strode forward, confidently and tied it to the collar. The man led, and Tempus followed, through the great building to a smaller room. At this new location, there was strange furniture including a large mat. Onto this he was led, the leash dropped to the floor. The man moved behind a large wooden structure and sat down, and then began doing something with a feather.

People came and went throughout the day, and Tempus watched. The visitors all gave him a wide birth, and the man in the seat seemed happy to see their discomfort at the sight of the massive beast.

In the evening a woman came with food, and he greedily devoured it. The man gave an order, and a soldier in armour came to take Tempus outside. There was an immense area with cut grass and carefully manicured trees. Tempus smelt the outside world in a way he hadn't experienced since he was young. This was freedom!

Over the next few weeks, he grew comfortable in his new life. The man in the seat would often take meetings, and Tempus was always there, sitting in his corner. He was well fed and exercised and had little to do except sleep. Was this his reward for a life of misery?

The black haired woman changed everything. She came to visit the seated man. He knew her well, greeted her by standing and kissing her on the cheek, but she took one look at Tempus, and he could tell she was afraid. Something in her smell told Tempus she was evil and he immediately disliked her. Over the next few days, the seated man spent less time in this room. The black-haired woman turned up with two men, and they stared at Tempus for some time. She held a slim dagger in her hand while the two men looked on, but something must have stayed her. Tempus growled and rose to his feet while her two companions drew swords, but she stilled them with a wave of her hand, and they left.

Sometime later the seated man came for him, leading him out of the room. He passed the leash to an armoured man and gave him orders, petting Tempus on the head as he did so. Led by his leash, he hopped into a wagon, though this time there was no cage.

He watched the countryside roll by, the scent of fresh air tickling his nose. He tried to stay awake to take in all the new sights and sounds, but his worn out body gave in, and he fell asleep. At night he rested while his escort lit a fire. The next morning they were up and travelling again. It continued like this for a few days until the wagon rolled into a little village and crossed over a small wooden bridge. Soon, they were approaching an estate lined with trees where a large white building was waiting for them.

"He arrived at Uxley," said Anna, recognizing the description.

"Yes," agreed Albreda, "his tale is almost done."

"But we know the rest," said Anna, "don't we?"

"Let her finish the tale, Anna," piped in Gerald. "I'd like to know how Tempus sees it."

"Very well," agreed Anna. "Please continue, Albreda."

His new home was enormous, and Tempus found endless fascination sniffing out all the nooks and crannies. The people here were fearful of him, but they gave him food and water and left him to his own devices. The servants kept visiting the upper floor and Tempus, intrigued, decided to investigate. He followed them one day to discover them entering a room. He sat at the end of the hallway, listening, only to hear the sounds of a young girl coming from within. He tried to get closer but was shooed away by servants with brooms.

He wondered if it was his old mistress from so long ago, but came to the conclusion it couldn't be, for too much time had passed. Who was this little girl? He took to wandering the hallway and soon decided this would be where he would sleep. He had failed to protect his mistress all those years ago, and his punishment was to be sent into a life of torment; he would never let it happen again!

Night after night he slept in the hall, keeping it safe, ever alert. The cold weather came and then the spring, and still, he held his vigil.

The weather warmed, and the windows were opened to allow a fresh breeze. It was the middle of the night, and Tempus was awoken by a strange smell - intruders! He was instantly awake and stood, sniffing the air. He detected distant footsteps treading softly; were the servants awake? He crouched in the darkness, his eyes glued to the little girl's door.

Movement down the hall caught his attention; something was approaching in the darkness. The girl's door began to open, and he realized with a shock that the intruders were dressed all in black. As the door swung open, Tempus attacked, launching himself at the closest target. His victim was caught completely unawares as the mastiff's powerful jaws snapped shut on the man's thigh. A terrifying scream erupted from his lips, and he fell to the floor, blood spurting everywhere as Tempus released his grip.

Other men went through the door, but one turned to face him, metal glinting in his hand. Tempus moved without thinking, clamping down on the forearm before the blade could swing. There was a snap of bone and Tempus released, thundering into the room to save his new mistress.

Two men were inside and the little girl, awoken by the commotion, was now sitting up in the bed, screaming. Onto the back of an intruder leaped Tempus, driving the man to the floor, his teeth sinking into the trespasser's neck. A violent wringing of his head was all it took to snap the bone, and he turned on the final invader.

The last man standing held a short blade. He stabbed at Tempus' face, but years of fighting had honed the great dog's reflexes, and he dodged it, turning his head to clamp down on the villain's forearm. Once again, the great jaws clenched, and the man let out a horrifying scream of agony.

Sounds erupted from all over the house, and Tempus turned to finish off the others. By the time the servants arrived, there were four dead bodies with buckets of blood covering the floor and walls. Horrified by the carnage, the servants swept the girl from the room, using brooms to chase off her protector. Back to the hallway, Tempus moved, pleased with his success. No longer would his mistress be in danger, he could now die easy, having fulfilled his obligation. Servants came and went, with buckets and mops, attempting to clearing away the remains of the awful carnage.

By next evening, the Hall was almost restored to its former state. Tempus sat, watching the door, lest more enemies appear. The little girl had been returned to her room, and he moved closer, so as not to be surprised again. It was now dark, the sun having disappeared, and he sat, listening to the sounds of the house. He knew the servants would soon be abed, and that was when there was the greatest danger. He must be vigilant.

Behind the door, the little girl was crying in her sleep, and he felt helpless, trapped as he was in the hallway. He barked once, to ward off any evil invaders, and then settled in for the long night. The crying stopped, and soon he heard the door creaking open. He stared into the darkness, watching for black-clad bandits, only to see the little yellow-haired girl in her nightgown, peering into the night.

She looked right at Tempus and waved him forward. He trotted quietly down the hall and entered the room, while the little girl closed the door behind him, and then climbed into bed.

Tempus lay on the floor at the foot of the bed, guarding the door. Soon, he heard his mistress's breathing slow down, and knew she was asleep. He sat and listened. Strange, he thought, to hear the sound after so many years. He heard her tossing and turning, and then unexpectedly there was the sound of her tears. He stood up, and walked over to the side of the bed, his massive head higher than the mattress.

The little girl was huddled in her blankets, shivering and Tempus felt such compassion for his helpless young mistress. He climbed onto the bed, his weight sinking the mattress on one side, and placed his paw on her arm. Her tossing subsided, and she fell into restful slumber.

-Interlude XIII-

BODDEN

Summer 960 MC

Anna hugged her faithful dog, "I'm so glad you were there, Tempus. I'll never let anything like that happen to you again."

"How old is he?" asked Hayley. "He's showing grey around his muzzle."

"He's quite old," responded Albreda, "though his healing at the hands of Andronicus has helped him immensely."

Fitz was startled, "The Royal Life Mage healed him? He wouldn't even heal Gerald."

"I suspect," offered Beverly, "that the request never even got to him."

"Valmar!" spat out her father.

"Precisely!" concurred Beverly.

"I don't understand why Valmar seems to hate you so much," commented Hayley.

"I do," said Gerald. "It's jealousy. Valmar is the marshal-general, but he'll never have the ability of the baron. He's the best commander in the kingdom and Valmar resents that."

"I'm afraid," offered Beverly, "that I didn't add to the family reputation during my time in the capital. The marshal-general and I didn't exactly see eye-to-eye."

"Well," offered Fitz, "I suppose he can rise to the level of his incompetency then."

They all laughed. It was good to be in such friendly company, where they could all talk freely.

"How long will Tempus live?" asked Anna, looking to Albreda for reassurance.

"I suspect for some time yet. He's here for a purpose; he has some task which must be completed before he passes to the Afterlife."

"Animals go to the Afterlife?" asked a surprised Anna.

Albreda looked at her with a smile, "Of course they do. The Gods made all the creatures, why wouldn't they see fit to reward them? It's pretty arrogant to think that only Humans could go to the Afterlife."

"So I'll see him there, one day," Anna said, comforted with the knowledge.

"He's not going to the Afterlife for some time," Albreda informed her. "He's still got you to protect, and you provide him with what he's always been searching for."

"What's that?"

"Love."

"Well," said Baron Fitzwilliam, rising to his feet, "it's getting quite late, and we have work to do tomorrow." He looked to Princess Anna, "You," he continued, "have to leave for Kingsford in the morning and the rest of us have to be up before you, to make sure everything's ready to go. I do wish you'd let me accompany you, Your Highness."

"Nonsense, Baron," replied Anna with a smile, "you're needed here, and besides, in a sense, part of you will be with me anyway."

The confused look on the baron's face made Anna chuckle, "Gerald and Beverly are both going with me, and you trained them."

The door opened, and Anna's maid Sophie entered, curtsying. "Your bed is all made up, Highness," she offered.

"I'll be up in a few moments, we've just been telling stories of the past," Anna informed her.

"What stories, Highness?" asked the young maid.

"The story of how Tempus came to Uxley," offered Gerald. "Though I suspect you'd be too young to remember that. When did you arrive at the Hall, Sophie?"

"A year or two before you did, Gerald," she answered. "Why do you ask?"

"It sounds like Tempus' arrival caused quite a stir. I wondered if you knew of it?"

"I do," said Sophie, "though I was only a young girl at the time. Hanson told me all about it."

"I would think" offered Beverly, "that the whole episode must have been awfully traumatic for such a young child."

"It was, miss. Hanson said if it hadn't been for Lady Felicia, the princess wouldn't have made it."

"Who's Lady Felicia?" asked Gerald.

"I assume," said the baron, "that she refers to the Queen's sister, Lady Felicia Warren. She died a number of years ago."

"I'd forgotten about her," added Anna. "I was so young, and I believe she only visited the once."

"It's true," said Sophie. "She arrived the summer after Tempus did."

"You must tell us more," begged Anna. "I'd love to know the full tale; I don't remember much."

"Yes, come along Sophie," remarked Gerald, rising to his feet. "Come and have a seat and tell us the story. Hayley, get her a drink, would you?"

Sophie sat down, looking woefully out of place. "It's not really my story, I was told it by Hanson," she protested.

"Never mind that," said Gerald, handing her some wine. "None of us here are expert storytellers."

"You are, Gerald," offered Anna. "You tell me stories all the time!"

Gerald blushed at the compliment, and the others smiled at his obvious affection for the princess. "Please continue," he prompted.

"Very well. It was the summertime, and it all started with a fancy carriage pulling up to Uxley Hall…"

A Visitor Comes to Uxley

UXLEY HALL

Summer 951 MC

T he carriage rolled up the path, bumping along on the uneven ground, its passenger peering out from behind the drawn curtains. Lady Felicia Warren looked out upon a disused estate that had fallen upon hard times. "A shame," she muttered out loud to herself, "that such a magnificent estate should be so ill-treated."

Stopping before the grand entrance, she waited patiently while her footman opened the door, placing a small step to help her down. She emerged into the sunlight, blinking at the unexpected brightness of the day. She watched as servants hastened to assemble by the door, and she pretended to straighten her dress to give them time to prepare. Looking up, she recognized Alistair Hanson standing at their head and smiled; it was good to see a familiar face. As she stepped forward, Hanson bowed.

"Nice to see you, Alistair," she said. "I trust Uxley has been good to you?"

"It has indeed, my lady," he returned.

"You can dismiss the servants," she commanded. "I'm sure they have more interesting things to do than greet an old lady. You and I, however, have things to discuss."

"Of course, my lady." He turned, dismissing the others with a wave of his hand, and then smiled back at Lady Felicia. "Shall I show you in?"

"By all means, Alistair. You can arrange for my things after we've spoken." The two began making their way into the Hall.

"I was surprised to hear news of your visit, my lady," the steward began. "It was not something I was expecting."

"There has been an attempt on the life of my niece," she retorted, perhaps a little more vehemently than she expected. "What else was I to do?"

"But surely the king-"

"The king has seen fit to do nothing, and my sister is just as bad. You would think that a mother would show up at the very least! Sorry Alistair, I know it's not your fault. I'm pleased that you have kept me informed."

"You insisted on it when you had me assigned here, my lady. Serving you and Lord Warren was an absolute pleasure."

"Thank you, Alistair; you always did have a flair for words. I knew when my husband died that you needed a change of scenery; this seemed just the place for you. I suspect you've been most diligent in your duties?"

"Of course, madam. Though I daresay this latest… tragedy is far out of my experience."

"And how is my young niece?"

"I'm afraid she is not doing well, my lady. She is very withdrawn and seldom comes out of her room. She also stays quite close to that beast the king sent down here."

"The dog? That's hardly surprising, considering what you wrote me."

"Shall I take you to meet her, madam?"

"No, I shall settle in and make my own introduction once I've done some investigating."

"Investigating? I didn't realize we were under suspicion," Hanson commented.

"And you aren't, my dear old friend. I merely want to get the staff's opinion of the situation before I move forward."

"And do you think there is hope for her? Perhaps the King's Life Mage can help?"

"The King's Life Mage likely doesn't even know she exists. His Majesty's command has seen to that. Honesty, I don't know why the king can't just acknowledge her!"

"I've afraid that is out of my control, my lady."

"Of course it is, Alistair. Now pour me a drink and have the servants unload my belongings. I shall have to think on this alone for a while."

"May I ask how long you will be staying?"

"As long as needed. I suspect, at the very least, I'll be here till the end of summer. I shouldn't like to be here when my sister arrives in the autumn; we still don't see eye-to-eye on certain matters."

"Very well, madam," said Hanson. "I will leave you in peace and have your luggage seen to."

It was early in the evening when Anna was brought before her aunt. She was led into the study by a middle-aged woman who was, ostensibly, her nanny. Lady Felicia was unimpressed by the dour look on the woman's face. Her young niece was pale, with big circles under her eyes. She was constantly wringing her hands and glancing about as if the very room was filled with monsters.

"You poor girl," Felicia said, reaching out to take the youngster's hand.

Her niece shrank back at the attempt. As her offer was withdrawn, Felicia couldn't help but notice the trembling in the young girl's hands.

"Where's the hound?" she asked.

"The filthy beast won't let us near him, my lady," replied the nanny. "The servants had to chase him off with brooms just to get the girl out of the room."

"Show me," she demanded, rising to her feet.

She was led upstairs to a long hallway. Midway down was the child's room, and upon arriving at the door, Felicia looked down to see a dark stain on the wooden floor. "Is this the room where the attack occurred?" she asked.

"Yes, my lady," replied the maid.

"Well for Saxnor's sake! This won't do. Have her moved immediately. It's no wonder the child is petrified with fear. Where's the dog?"

"Inside, miss."

Felicia opened the door slowly, peering inside to see a large mastiff pacing the room. It was by the window, and when it turned to face her direction, she saw that there was dried blood all over the creature's muzzle and chest.

"Has no one seen fit to wash down the poor thing?"

"No one can get near him, madam. The beast is a killer."

"Nonsense! He's just protective towards the young girl. Go and get me a wash bowl and cloth," she commanded. With the door open the rest of the way, she noticed the room was quite large, and there were stains on the sheets, likely dried blood from the hound.

"This will never do," she uttered.

She strode into the room advancing directly towards the dog. It stopped its movement, eyeing her suspiciously. She reached out with her hand, allowing it to sniff her, and then began to pet its head.

"You poor creature," she said. "All you were doing was protecting the child, and this is how they treat you."

A maid appeared with a bowl and cloth. Felicia sat in front of the hound and rolled up her sleeves. Dipping the cloth in the water, she began gently wiping the dried blood off the animal's muzzle. It was thick and crusty, and it took some effort, but the beast did not object, and before long she saw a clean, scarred face staring back at her.

"There," she exclaimed, "much better!"

She turned to speak to the maid and saw other servants lurking behind, "My niece will be moved to the room at the end of the hallway, across from the library. Bring her back here, and I shall walk her and her pet down to their new room myself."

There were mutterings of obedience while the servants started removing clothes from the room, giving the dog a wide berth. Anna arrived shortly after that, the small pale child holding onto Hanson's hand.

"Here she is, madam."

"Come, child," she said in a soothing voice. "Let us take you and your faithful companion to your new room." She held out her hand for her niece and was rewarded by a timid advance. Lady Felicia remained kneeling beside the dog as this occurred. "Have you a name for your dog?" she asked.

The little girl shook her head. Felicia looked at Hanson who replied, "There's a plaque on his collar, madam."

She gazed at the brass plate where 'Tempus' was emblazoned. Looking back at Anna, she said, "His name's Tempus. Can you say that?"

The little girl nodded, squeaking out a reply, "Tempus."

"Yes, my dear, that's right." Felicia smiled, rising slowly to her feet. "Now, let's get you out of this place, with its unpleasant memories." She held out her hand and waited, patiently, while Anna took it. "Come along, Tempus," she said, casting her gaze in the direction of the dog. The creature must have known his name, for he advanced slowly, following their footsteps.

Down the hall, she led them, an army of servants preceding them. Anna walked slowly, Felicia letting her set the pace. By the time they arrived at her new room, the servants were exiting, the newly laid bed ready for her arrival.

"This is going to be your new room, Anna," Felicia said. "You and Tempus will sleep here. You're right across from the library. Now, let's get you ready for bed, it's getting late."

She called in the nanny to change her niece into her night clothes and left them to it.

Later that evening, Lady Felicia peered into her niece's room. The child was asleep, tossing and turning, the dog, Tempus, lying beside her. The poor thing was reliving the attack, she thought, something must be done to occupy her mind. She resolved to talk it over with Hanson in the morning, to see if he had any ideas. Making her way back down the hall to where her own room lay, she took no more than a few dozen steps when a thought crossed her mind, and so she wheeled about, heading in the direction of the library.

The library at Uxley Hall was well stocked, which surprised her. The current king was not known as a great reader, and she imagined that his ancestors must have been better educated. She had spent time in the company of King Andred IV, and had been less than impressed with his intelligence; whatever her sister saw in him was a complete mystery. She had warned Elenor that the king would lose interest in her, but her sister wouldn't listen. Of course, after giving birth to three children, the king took a mistress and then the biggest shock of all; the queen became pregnant. The poor child was banished to this estate, to spend her whole life in isolation.

Felicia knew her sister was ashamed of the product of her affair. Elenor had always been the prim and proper one, but seldom took responsibilities for her actions. In a way, it had been inevitable. Once she lost the love of the king, she was bound to find it elsewhere, for Elenor was a woman that constantly needed attention and comfort. Felicia herself had never been blessed with children and was furious that her sister would treat this child so callously. She was now taking it upon herself to see that Anna was provided for; given the life which she deserved.

She was thinking this through as she perused the books which occupied the shelves. There was all manner of titles here, though most were made for adults. She picked a book of fables from the shelf and read over its contents; short stories, all in a steady hand. They had been written in the early days of Merceria, and were collectively known as the Mercerian Fables. The author had been a Holy Father of the church, and he had taken great pains to illustrate the tome with pictures. Satisfied with her choice, she settled down into a large chair to read through it. It proved to be the perfect bedtime choice for no sooner had she started reading it than her eyes began to droop just before she nodded off.

Felicia awoke with a sore neck, the book lying on the floor at her feet. Cursing her behaviour, she made her way out into the hall. The early morning sun peered through the windows, illuminating her way. Hearing the servants scurrying about below, she quickly made her way to her room, jumping into bed to cover her activity. No sooner had she pulled up the sheets than there was a rap at the door. She bid them enter, and in came a maid, carrying a tray with a bowl and water, along with a towel for a morning wash.

"I shall take my morning meal in the dining room," Felicia instructed. "Please have Hanson join me." The young maid bowed respectfully and disappeared from view.

Making her way into the dining hall, Felicia sat at the table as the servants brought food and drink. The smell of fresh bread seemed to permeate the household, reminding her of own youth, so many years ago. She had lived a long life and yet, had so little to mark the passing of her years.

A servant came in with a plate of freshly sliced bread and honey, and she cast her eyes appreciatively over it. She was about to ask Lord Warren if he wanted some and then remembered... he had died. She dropped the bread back on the plate, her appetite forgotten. Honey had always been his favourite. She felt tears forming in her eyes as her loneliness increased.

"I must keep busy," she said, wiping her eyes with a handkerchief. "There must be a way to help Anna."

There was a light tap on the door. Felicia composed herself and then beckoned the visitor to enter.

The door opened to reveal Alistair Hanson, "You called, my lady?"

"I did, Alistair. Come and sit down."

Hanson knew better than to refuse and so he took a seat beside her.

"Have some bread, my dear old friend," she bid.

"Are you not hungry, madam?"

"I was, but now I've changed my mind."

Hanson took a tentative bite of the bread, swallowing it quickly before speaking, "Is there something, in particular, you wanted to talk to me about, madam?"

"Yes, Alistair. Our young ward is having nightmares."

"Can you blame her?"

"No, but we must divert her attention, occupy her mind. I was thinking that I might start reading to her. You know her better than I, do you think she would like that?"

Hanson grimaced, "I'm afraid I can't say, my lady. The king has left rather explicit instructions. We are not to coddle the child."

"Hah!" exclaimed Lady Felicia. "I thought as much. Well, you can be sure I will ignore the pompous ass. I shall make it my job to coddle the child as much as I can. What does she do?"

"Do, madam?"

"Yes, Alistair. What does she do all day? Surely she must do something?"

"I'm afraid she doesn't do much of anything, my lady. She spends most of the day in her room, especially since the attack."

"Does she walked the grounds?"

"No," the steward replied, "I'm afraid not."

"Has the child been completely ignored?" she exclaimed.

"I must apologize again, my lady, but the king's orders-"

"Yes, I know. The king's orders are explicit. Frankly, I'm surprised he didn't have her eliminated, he seems the type."

Hanson paled at the remark. It wasn't wise to talk about the king in such a manner, but Lady Felicia Warren was of an age and cared little for such things.

"Perhaps," he suggested, "you might see fit to make these changes yourself, madam. Naturally, should these new rules be put in place, we would be expected to continue with them once you left."

Felicia smiled, "Why Hanson, you old rogue, how clever of you!"

"When would you like to start, my lady?"

"I think I shall start this evening. I want to walk the grounds today, see for myself how they look. I shouldn't like to take her out only to get caught in a bog. I'll take a couple of servants with me, perhaps a coachman or two. Do you have a groundskeeper?"

"I'm afraid not. We haven't had one in years, there's been no need. The king hasn't visited since Anna was brought here."

"When was the last time my sister was here?"

"She comes once a year, usually to coincide with the young girl's birthday."

"Usually?"

"I'm afraid she's rather erratic in her schedule, my lady."

"Somehow that doesn't surprise me. Elenor always was a little flighty."

"What do you want us to do with her today?"

"Please keep an eye on her. I'll be interested to know if she's any different now that she's in a new room. Just keep to her regular schedule for now."

"Yes, my lady," the steward replied, rising to his feet. "Will there be anything else, madam?"

"No, that's all for now, Alistair."

The grounds of the estate proved to be a bounty of flowers and plants. Lady Felicia wandered the fields taking in all the smells and sights she could. It had been years since she had been out in this manner and her body, used to the life of complacency to which she had become familiar, complained at the exertion. She returned to the Hall exhausted but pleased with her discoveries.

That evening she visited young Anna as the girl was tucked into bed, the faithful dog lying on the floor beside her. Felicia entered, pulling a chair over beside her niece.

"Hello, Anna," she said. "I thought you might like a bedtime story. Do you know what that is?"

She shook her head. "No," she whispered.

"I'm going to read you a story. It's from a book of fables. Fables are made up stories that teach lessons. Are you ready?"

Anna pulled the blankets up close to her face, and Felicia could see a look of fear.

"Why don't we have Tempus jump up here with you?" she asked.

The young girl nodded her head. Felicia pat her hand on the bed, and the great beast leaped up. It was a strange sight, for the mastiff was many times larger than the young girl. The dog wiggled his way up beside her, shaking the bed as he did so, until Anna's hand rested comfortably on his head.

"There," said Felicia. "Tempus is all ready for the story to begin. Are you?

The child solemnly nodded her head.

"This story is called 'The Mermaid of Colbridge.' It takes place in the great city which bears that name, on a river that leads to the Great Sea of Storms…"

It was late at night by the time Felicia made her way back to her own room. The child had fretted, and she wondered if, perhaps, the story had been too much for her, but she finally fell asleep. She had crept out of the room to the sounds of a snoring dog and a little girl who murmured in her sleep.

Lady Felicia woke early the next day, but her body was not up to the task at hand. It was almost noon by the time she felt ready to take Anna on a walk, and she feared she might not have the energy to return once they were done. She fortified herself with a glass of wine and made her way to Anna's room. Her niece stood by the window, staring out toward the front of the estate. As Felicia entered, the child turned along with Tempus, who wagged his tail as he did so.

"Good morning," bid Felicia. "I trust you've slept well?"

Anna nodded.

"Good. And how has Tempus been? Is he well?"

Again a nod.

She knelt down by her niece, to look at her at her own level. "Now come, my child. When I ask you a question, you must answer with your words. Let's try again, shall we? Did you sleep well?"

"Yes," the little girl responded.

"Excellent! Now I don't know about you, but I suspect our friend Tempus here would like a nice walk outside. What do you think? Shall we let take him?"

There was that fearful look on Anna's face again, and so Felicia switched tactics, "I bet if we had Tempus run down the hall he'd scare the servants. Shall we give it a try?" There it was, the briefest of smiles. Progress!

"Come along then," said Felicia, attempting to rise. Her knees were sore, and she struggled, using the window sill to steady herself. "These old bones aren't what they used to be."

Anna reached out, grasping the older woman's hand. "Me too?" she asked.

"Why, of course, dear. We shall all go for a walk, but let's give your friend the run of the hallway first, shall we?"

They entered the hallway, and Felicia stood, gazing down the long corridor. They were on the upper floor, populated by children's bedrooms, though only one was in use. It was the perfect place for Tempus to run back and forth, but she had no stick to toss to coax the dog into action. She cast her eyes about, finally settling on her young niece. The faithful beast was sitting to her side, her hand resting gently on the creature's back.

"I have an idea, Anna," she said, making her decision. "But first you must learn to call him. Can you say 'Tempus'?"

"Tempus," the girl replied.

"Excellent. Now try again, this time a little louder," she prompted.

"Tempus!" Anna yelled, to be greeted by a bark. There was the briefest moment of silence from the girl, as the sound echoed throughout the mansion, and then her niece giggled.

"Now you wait here, young Anna, while I make my way to the other end of the hall." She walked down with slow, deliberate steps, then paused a moment before turning to face the others. "Come, Tempus!" she commanded. "Come here, boy."

Tempus barked again, shaking the very walls with his exuberance, and then pounded down the hallway, screeching to a halt in front of the old lady. Felicia smiled, patting him on the head, "Now it's your turn, Anna. Call him!"

"Tempus!" yelled Anna, only to be rewarded with the great beast wheeling about and thundering down the hall once more. He came to a halt just in front of the girl, and she buried her face in his chest, throwing her arms around him as she laughed.

"That's it," exclaimed Felicia. "Now send him back again. Come along Tempus, come to Aunt Felicia!"

Back and forth ran the giant dog, each time threatening to shake the foundation loose.

There was a commotion from downstairs, and soon they heard footsteps coming up the stairs in the great hall. Felicia walked back to Anna, Tempus following at a more sedate pace. A moment later she saw Hanson appear around the corner, along with a footman.

"Is there something wrong, Alistair?" she asked.

"There was a loud noise, my lady. We feared something might be amiss."

Felicia looked at her niece, "I didn't hear anything, did you, Anna?"

Anna shook her head.

"There, you see, Alistair? You must be imagining things."

Alistair knew something was up, but he kept silent, relaxing into a less agitated pose. "Might I enquire as to your plans for the day, madam?" he asked.

"I think we shall go outdoors; the dog needs a bit of exercise. Come along, Anna, it's time we let this dog of yours stretch his legs." She held out her hand, waiting for the child to grasp it, and then proceeded toward the great hall and the grand staircase.

Anna tried to stop her. "Other stairs," she said.

Felicia stopped walking and knelt to look at the young girl from her own height once again, "You are a princess, Anna. You use the grand staircase here. This is your home, you're not a servant. Besides, Tempus here is too large, we don't want him getting stuck on the stairs, do we?"

Her niece shook her head.

"Use your words, Anna," she encouraged.

"No," Anna replied.

Felicia rose again, her knees once more complaining from the strain. They made their way to the grand staircase. The second floor of the great hall was in the centre of the building. It was a large, two-storey affair, but the builders had constructed a balcony that ran around the perimeter, allowing those present to gaze down to the great room below. To one side was the wide staircase, built of sturdy oak and said to be of Dwarven construction. Felicia rolled her eyes at the thought. Whenever something was well built, it was always attributed to Dwarves, as if Humans were incapable of such things. She halted them at the top of the stairs. "Go to the bottom of the stairs, Anna," she commanded, "and then we'll have Tempus run down them. Do you understand?"

"Yes," Anna replied. She rushed down the stairs in a hurry, and for a moment Felicia was worried she might stumble and fall, but in a thrice, her niece was at the bottom, facing upward.

"Back up a little, Anna," said Felicia. "He's a large dog, he'll need room to slow down."

The young girl did as she was bid, and then looked up, expectantly.

"Call him now, Anna," yelled Felicia.

"Tempus," yelled Anna, her small voice echoing through the large room. The great beast rushed down the stairs, drawing to a halt before his young mistress, his tail wagging and his tongue hanging out.

"Come back, Tempus," called Felicia, and the great dog turned to rush back up the stairs, his feet tapping away at the steps like a drumbeat as he made his ascent.

Anna called again, and her aunt saw the smile as she watched. Tempus rushed back, eager in his new mode of play. Back and forth he ran as Felicia and Anna each took their turn calling him. Soon, servants appeared, lurking in the doorways to observe this strange behaviour. Finally, the great dog made one last run down to Anna, and Felicia took pity on him. The poor creature was winded, and though his tail was still wagging, he was moving slower, tired from his exertions.

Felicia made her way down the stairs to pet Tempus, who now lay on his back, his legs curled above him. Anna was rubbing his belly, and the dog's tongue seemed to fall out of his mouth.

"We must get him some water, I think," mused Felicia. "There's a trough out the side of the house, let's take him there."

She led them out through the front foyer, into the warmth of the noonday sun. Anna followed obediently, drawn by the excitement of playing with her dog. They rounded the side of the house and Tempus made a beeline for the trough, lapping up water in huge gulps. His thirst quenched, he trotted back to young Anna.

"Now," pondered Felicia, "we shall need a stick of some sort. Big enough to throw for Tempus, he's a large dog and needs his exercise."

"Exercise?" said Anna.

"Why, yes. He needs to stretch his legs, it helps him stay healthy. Come along, we'll see what's nearby."

She led her niece into the field which lay to the north of the Hall. Many years ago it had been the estate grounds, neatly trimmed and decorated with trees and bushes, but now it was a riot of brush, weeds and long, wild grass.

"Like this?" yelled Anna, hefting a small branch.

"Perfect," called out Felicia. "Now wave it at Tempus to get his attention, and then throw it."

Anna did as she was bid, only to be rewarded with a bark. Tempus disappeared into the long grass, reappearing moments later, the branch held firmly in his mouth.

Felicia enjoyed seeing the wonderment on her niece's face. Anna took hold of the stick with one hand and pulled in an effort to remove it from his mouth. Tempus simply let go of it and Anna, expecting more resistance, fell to the ground, landing on her bottom. There was a loud laugh as she jumped to her feet, to repeat the toss.

Felicia found a fallen branch to sit on while she watched with fascination. Always one to enjoy hounds, it made her think of her own youth, so many years ago. She had wanted children, and watching her niece brought her pangs of joy mixed with sadness. This is all the family I have now, she thought. Elenor was never the same after marrying the king. She spent her days in seclusion, refusing to see the rest of her family. Felicia fought back bitter tears. The king had forbidden her to visit her other niece, Margaret, and the two princes as well. Perhaps he feared her power, for her husband had been an influential man at court in the days before Andred took the throne.

She was shaken back to reality when Anna ran up to her.

"I'm hungry," the young girl complained.

"Well, I imagine I would be too if I'd been running back and forth like you. Come along, it's time we eat." She led her back into the Hall, leaving her reminiscences behind.

That evening she read Anna another fable and tucked her in for the night. She pat Tempus on the head and quietly left the room, intent on visiting the library again, but then remembered falling asleep on the chair and decided that morning might be a better time for such things. She made her way downstairs to fortify herself with a drink before bed, only to run into Hanson.

"Can I get you anything, my lady?" he asked.

"I think a drink is in order, Alistair," she said. "I'm aching all over."

"I trust the day went well, madam?"

"It did, indeed. We shall try making more progress tomorrow."

"Shall I bring you a drink in the trophy room?"

"Yes, a wonderful idea. Once I'm done, I want to peer in on Anna and see how she's sleeping."

"Do you want me to escort you?" he asked.

"To the trophy room? Don't be absurd. I know my way around, you just fetch that drink."

"Yes, madam."

Fortified by a stiff drink, she made her way back to her niece's room, opening the door to peer inside and see little Anna fast asleep.

"So," she muttered aloud, "no tossing and turning this evening. It appears we have made some progress."

"I'm sorry," said a voice, behind her. "Did you say something, my lady?"

She turned to see a young maid, "No, I was just thinking out loud. Pay no attention." She made her way back to her room, settling in for the night.

Felicia resolved to take Anna on a tour of the estate the next day. This time she rose early and had everything ready to go. She entered Anna's room as the servants woke her, and spoke while the maid dressed the young girl, "We're going on a look-see today, Anna."

"Look-see?" queried her niece.

"Yes, we're going to walk the estate. I'll show you all the land hereabouts. I think you'll find it most engrossing. I've arranged for a meal to be prepared. We shall meet the servants on the hill overlooking the northeast fields. Now, we need to get you going, it's a long way from here, and we still have to find some sticks for Tempus."

Anna hurried into her clothes, and then they headed downstairs to breakfast. Tempus, picking up on the excitement, barked out loud, charging ahead of them. The meal was a rush, and then they were out of the Hall, into the fresh, warm, summer air. The sky was clear, and the sweet fragrance of flowers drifted across the fields. Tempus ran ahead, dashing from side to side as he heard the sounds of birds calling.

Anna was entranced and wandered the field alongside her aunt, her head turning all about at the sheer wonderment of it all. They stopped from time to time, and Felicia showed her some of the flowers that she recalled from her own youth, so very long ago. As she had arranged, noon brought them to a small hill overlooking the grounds. Hanson was already there, along with a handful of other servants who had carried the food. The two of them sat on small wooden chairs, looking into the distance as they ate their meal.

"This is your home, Anna. All that you see around you is part of Uxley." She could almost see her younger self, frolicking in the tall grass, chasing after her little sister, Elenor. Life had been joyous, and she wished she could return to those happier days.

Tempus barked, and Anna pointed at him, "Look," she cried out.

Tempus was wagging his tail, chasing a butterfly, drawing Felicia back to the present. These are happier days, she thought. For too long I've grieved for the loss of my husband. It's time to embrace life, to live the life I would like, she decided.

Lady Felicia rose to her feet. "Come along, Anna," she called. "It's time to give Tempus a hand."

Through the grass, the two ran, down the hill, following the dog's trail. Their elusive prey vanished from view, and they rushed back up the hill to collapse on the ground, their eyes staring up at the sky.

"Are you all right?" queried Hanson.

"I'm fine, Alistair," she answered, gasping for breath. "Just a bit winded." She rolled onto her side to look at her niece. "Oh Anna, isn't it wonderful? This is just like when I was a little girl."

"Here?" asked Anna.

"Not here, but back in Kingsford, where I grew up. My sister and I used to run across the fields whenever we could. My family had a small estate just on the outskirts of town. Your grandfather raised horses, did you know that?"

"Clouds are beginning to roll in," observed Alistair. "Might I suggest we reschedule the rest of the walk in favour of another day?"

"An excellent suggestion, Alistair. Come along Anna, we must hasten back to the Hall, or we'll get wet."

By the time they returned, the rain had started and Lady Felicia, soaked head to foot, laughed in delight as they entered the structure. Only a few short days ago she would have been furious to get wet in such a manner, but now all she could do was look at her niece, the delight evident on her face. This was life, she thought.

Trips across the estate became more frequent with time, and by the end of summer, the entire household had become accustomed to Lady Felicia's presence. It was a joyous place to work and barely a day would pass without seeing smiles cross the faces of even the lowest of scullery maids. It was a sad day in early autumn when she finally decided it was time to leave. The servants assembled by the entrance as Lady Felicia came down to enter her carriage. Hanson held his arm out for her to steady herself for, despite her activity, her health was tenuous, at best.

She paused by the carriage door as Hanson spoke, "Must you leave, my lady?"

"I'm afraid so," she replied. "It has been an absolute pleasure to be here, Alistair, but my health is getting worse, and I don't want Anna to see me in decline. I said my goodbyes inside, better for her to remember me as I am now."

"We shall miss you, madam," he declared.

"As I shall miss you all," she responded. "Look after her, Alistair, she is our future."

"I will, madam," he promised.

She entered the carriage, the door closed behind her, and the driver hopped up to the front. The carriage pulled away, and Alistair Hanson watched as it bounced on its way.

The room was silent save for the scurrying of a quill across paper. Alistair Hanson dipped it once more into the ink and resumed his fine handiwork. There was a knock on the door, and he bid them enter. The door opened to reveal the face of Harris, one of the footmen.

"A letter has arrived, Sir," he said.

"That's odd," remarked Hanson. "It's not the usual day for such things." He looked up to contemplate the document being offered. "Thank you, Harris. That will be all."

The footman nodded, exiting the room quietly.

Hanson turned the letter over, examining the outside. It was a folded parchment, bearing a wax seal which he didn't recognize. The words 'Alistair Hanson - Uxley Hall' were written in a careful hand across its front. It was thick for such a letter, and he wondered if there might, perchance, be another enclosed within. He took his knife and, laying the letter on the table, carefully pried open the seal. Sure enough, inside was another letter, along with a small note. He looked at the smaller letter first, laying it flat in front of him.

Alistair Hanson,

It is with the greatest regret that I must inform you that Lady Felicia Warren has, this past month, passed from this life. She had been ill for some time and left this world in the greatest of comforts. In accordance with her instructions, I have forwarded the enclosed note for your perusal. Though I am unaware of the contents of the letter, she was most explicit in her demands. Funds should be arriving within a fortnight, pursuant to her arrangements. If you should happen to require assistance in any manner, please feel free to contact me,

Your obedient servant,

Jason Wendel

He looked at the name carefully, but it meant nothing to him. He glanced down at the second letter, instantly recognizing Lady Felicia's handwriting. Breaking the seal, he unfolded it, knowing it would be her last communication.

My dear Alistair,

I know I am not long for this world and the exertions of the last few months have proven to be most burdensome. I have taken it upon myself to make arrangements for my niece, Anna, for I know my sister well, and I fear that one day her interest in her own offspring will wane. I am aware that these instructions may place you at odds with the orders of the king, Alistair, and yet I hope that you can see, in your heart, that they are the right thing to do.

Anna deserves a life, not to be locked up in a stuffy old house. I beg you to make sure she is looked after properly. You have been a loyal servant for many years, my friend, but I would ask this last favour of you. Ignore the king when you can, she needs love and attention. The king will likely never acknowledge her, so I beseech you to treat her as you would any other child, with decency and respect. I have arranged an annual stipend for you. This is not to be recorded anywhere and may be used at your discretion. I can only hope that, with time, she will find friends and colleagues that she can count on, as I know I can count on you.

Farewell Alistair, may you find happiness and prosperity in your life. I leave mine now, knowing that my time on this world has not been wasted.

Lady Felicia Warren.

Alistair Hanson carefully folded the letter back up, and then stared at it for a few moments. He rose, making his way to the bookshelf, to withdraw a small wooden box, which he set on the desk. He opened it, placing the letter within, with exaggerated tenderness, closing the lid as quietly as he could. A tear ran down from his eye, and he let it remain, tracking its way to his chin, then he placed the box back upon the shelf.

"Goodbye, Lady Felicia," he said. "You will be sorely missed."

Finale

BODDEN

Summer 960 MC

≈

"Fascinating," mused Gerald. "I'd always wondered where the princess got her love of books from. Tell me, my lord, did you know Lady Warren?"

"I only met her once," said Fitz. "I was in the capital, long before I became baron. Edward and I were staggering about town, a little the worse for wear."

"That must have been when you met Mother," piped in Beverly.

"It was indeed. Edward and I were completely soused. We came out of the Boars Head and tried to climb into her carriage."

"Why would you do that?" asked Beverly.

"Well, we were drunk. One doesn't usually make good choices when one is inebriated."

"So what happened?" asked Hayley.

"As far as I could tell, not much. Lady Warren seemed amused at our fumblings, but her husband was outraged. He ordered us out of the carriage, and then made us stand by the roadside while he lectured us."

"Couldn't you have just left, my lord?" asked Gerald.

"Of course! But Lord Warren was an imposing figure. They say he could break a man just by staring at him. He tore into us and then told us to piss off. Edward and I couldn't contain ourselves, for you see Lord Warren was a most proper noble. To hear him utter those words 'piss off' was just too much to take. We ran as fast as we could, but our laughter must have enraged him for he came after us. Luckily, we lost him after a few blocks, and it was as we caught our breath that Edward decided he wanted to pay a call on a young lady he had met earlier in our visit. That's when I met your mother."

"Astounding," exclaimed Gerald. "I never knew you to be like that, my lord. I always pictured you as the perfect example of nobility."

"And of course I am," Fitz grinned. "Now it's getting late, and you lot have to be up early in the morning."

"Most assuredly, my lord," said Gerald turning to the princess, only to find her fast asleep.

"It appears some of us have already succumbed," uttered the baron. "Perhaps we should get her to bed?" He looked to Sophie, who began making her way toward the princess.

"I've got her, Sophie," said Gerald.

"Isn't she becoming a burden, now that she's grown?" asked Beverly.

"Never," said a resolute Gerald, "she could never be a burden." He lifted her gently, Tempus shifting ever so slightly to enable it. He rose, straightening his back. Beverly saw the effort required, for Anna had grown in the last few months and Gerald was getting no younger, but the look of determination on his face said it all; this was his honour and his alone.

Beverly rose, stretching as she did so, "This may be the last time in a long while that we're gathered all together like this."

"Then let us have one last toast to remember the occasion," said Fitz, raising his glass. "To old friends and new. No matter where you go, your friends shall be with you in your heart!"

The Mermaid of Colbridge

A Mercerian Fable

A long time ago, when the kingdom was in its infancy, the city of Colbridge was a great port. Ships and boats would make their way down the river, past the ancient swamp, to the sea of storms where all manner of strange creatures lived.

In the city lived two brothers, Aiden and Caiden, who were fishermen by trade. Every morning, before the sun was up, they would launch their boat on the riverbank and sail downstream to fish near the mouth of the river. Here they would cast out their net, letting it sink to the depths, to be pulled back in with its haul.

Three times they cast their net, each time bringing up a meagre haul.

"This is not working," complained Aiden.

"There are not enough fish here," agreed Caiden. "Let us go further out into the water and try again."

They sailed out onto the sea, always keeping the shore carefully in sight. They saw an old wreck of a ship, out on the rocks, its masts jutting from the water.

"Let's fish near that," said Aiden.

"Yes," agreed Caiden. "There will likely be lots of fish near the wreck, they would use it as a home."

They approached the ship, careful to keep their distance.

"Cast the net," said Aiden, and his brother threw it out as far as he could.

The net sank beneath the waves while Caiden held the hand line. A moment later, he pulled it in to reveal a copious deposit of fish.

"Do it again," said Aiden.

"We have enough to eat," said Caiden.

"We can sell the rest at market," said Aiden, and so Caiden, once again, cast the net.

The net sank beneath the waves, and then Caiden began pulling on the hand line to retrieve their haul. He emptied the contents onto the small boat, and the fish flopped around their feet.

"Perfect," said Caiden, "now we have plenty to eat and some to sell."

"Cast again," said Aiden, "for the haul is bountiful and we can sell even more."

For a third time, Caiden cast the net, dutifully holding onto the hand line. The net sank beneath the waves, but when he tried to pull it back in, he found it resisting. "There's something heavy in the net," said Caiden.

"Let me help you," said Aiden.

Together, they pulled on the hand line, and as the net drew near the surface, they saw a most wondrous sight, for before them, trapped in their net, was a mermaid with scintillating blue scales and hair the colour of gold.

"It's a mermaid!" exclaimed Caiden.

"We must kill it!" yelled Aiden, grabbing an oar. "Mermaids are evil!"

Aiden leaned over the side of the boat, using the oar as a club and began striking the mermaid.

The mermaid wailed in pain, and the scream carried out across the water.

"Stop!" yelled Caiden. "You're hurting it!"

"No," yelled Aiden, "it's evil and must be destroyed.

Caiden tried to stop his brother by grabbing the oar, and they struggled for control. The tiny boat was upset, and they lost their balance, both falling into the water.

The oar floated away as they struggled to swim in the rough waves. The hand line, now forgotten, sank beneath the waves, releasing the net. The brothers tried to swim to their boat, but the heavy waves of the sea drove it away from them.

Soon the waves were swirling around them, and Caiden looked at his brother to see the mermaid appear behind him. She rose, waist high, out of the water and placed her hands on his brother's shoulders. A moment later they both disappeared beneath the waves, with only a few bubbles of air rising to the surface.

Caiden swam faster, but the boat was still floating away. He heard the sound of rippling water and turned to see the mermaid behind him. She gazed into his eyes and he floated, mesmerized as the mermaid put her arms beneath his and rolled under the water. A moment later he was being pulled across the surface. He looked up to see the boat, within easy reach. Caiden hauled himself aboard and then looked back at the water.

The mermaid was treading water at the side of the boat.

"Why did you kill my brother?" asked Caiden.

"He was mean," she said, "and wanted to kill me.

"And why did you save me?" Caiden asked.

"You tried to help me and saved my life. You should always treat others the way you would like to be treated," she responded, then dove beneath the waves, never to be seen again.

~

Cast of Characters

Albreda: Druid of the Whitewood and close friend and ally to Baron Richard Fitzwilliam.

Baron Richard 'Fitz' Fitzwilliam: Baron of Bodden and father to Dame Beverly Fitzwilliam. Mentor to Gerald Matheson, his former Sergeant-at-Arms.

Dame Beverly Fitzwilliam: Knight of the Hound and daughter of Baron Richard Fitzwilliam. Trained by Gerald Matheson and sworn into service with Princess Anna.

Dame Hayley Chambers: Former King's Ranger and now a Knight of the Hound sworn to serve Princess Anna.

Gerald Matheson: Former Sergeant-at-Arms to Baron Richard Fitzwilliam and close confidant to Princess Anna.

Princess Anna of Merceria: Second daughter and fourth child to Queen Elenor of Merceria. Third in line to the throne since the death of her brother, Prince Alfred.

Sophie: Princess Anna's personal maid and confident.

Tempus: A large Kurathian Mastiff and loyal pet of Princess Anna.

Share your thoughts!

If you enjoyed this book, share your favourite part! These positive reviews encourage other potential readers to give the series a try and help the book to populate when people are searching for a new fantasy series. And the best part is, each review I receive inspires me to write more in the land of Merceria and beyond.

Thank you!

How to get Battle at the River for free

Paul J Bennett's newsletter members are the first to hear about upcoming books, along with receiving exclusive content and Work In Progress updates.

Join the newsletter and receive *Battle at the River*, a Mercerian Short Story for free: PaulJBennettAuthor.com/newsletter

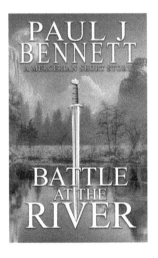

An enemy commander. A skilled tactician. Only one can be victorious.

The Norland raiders are at it again. When the Baron of Bodden splits their defensive forces, Sergeant Gerald Matheson thinks that today is a day like any other, but then something is different. At the last moment, Gerald recognizes the warning signs, but they are outnumbered, outmaneuvered, and out of luck. How can they win this unbeatable battle?

If you like intense battle scenes and unexpected plot twists, then you will love Paul J Bennett's tale of a soldier who thinks outside the box.

Heart of the Crown: Chapter 1

ALRIC

Spring 960 MC

The dancers moved in harmony across the floor, their slow, measured steps carried out in perfect unison. They were ablaze with colour, for the noble lords and ladies of the Kingdom of Weldwyn vied to outdo each other with their finery.

Alric was not impressed. He sat, watching their movements, bored with the majesty of it, his young mind filled rather with thoughts of combat and glory. His musings were rudely interrupted.

"Alric, did you hear me?"

He glanced up to see the face of his mother, Queen Igraine, looming down on him in disapproval.

"Sorry, Mother," he answered.

"Don't sorry me, we have guests to attend to. I know you're young, but you're still a prince, and you have responsibilities."

"To do what? Dance with the young ladies?"

His mother's frown grew increasingly intense, and he knew he had overstepped. "Sorry, Mother, it's just that they're all so..."

"So what?" she pressed.

"Sycophantic?"

"Well, what do you expect? You're fifteen, Alric. Your brothers were both engaged by your age."

"That's not fair, Mother. Alstan is the heir, he had no choice, and you picked out Cuthbert's wife when he was only six." He watched her face soften but knew what was about to come.

"I'm sorry, Alric," she said. "I know it's a burden, but we are royals, we have responsibilities."

"And what, exactly, are my responsibilities?"

"We will have to see," she said, avoiding the answer, as always. "Now, let's get you onto the dance floor, shall we? You have an impression to make."

He knew he was defeated, as always, but he could never stay upset with his mother for long. Rising to his feet, he straightened his tunic and was about to step onto the dance floor when the music stopped, the melody complete. He glanced about desperately, anything to avoid the attention of Lady Julianne, who was now walking toward him. His eyes rested on his oldest brother, and he moved toward the eldest prince with purpose. Lady Julianne tried to talk to him, but he pretended not to hear and strode past, ignoring her entirely.

"Alstan," he called out.

Prince Alstan was standing in a small knot of people and turned upon hearing his name. His face lit up. "Alric? What is it?"

The young prince had kept walking until he was directly in front of his brother, but now words failed him. He had been so eager to avoid the attention of the young lady that he had stumbled into what perhaps might be an even more embarrassing moment. He glanced back over his shoulder to see Julianne bearing down on him, and he felt a moment of panic.

"Court," he blurted out, "something about the court."

Alstan knit his brows, "I'm surprised you heard about that. I didn't think you had an interest in such things."

Now that Alric was part of the conversation, he dove in, desperate to avoid the unpleasant encounter he had run from. "I was quite fascinated," he said, trying to sound like he knew what he was talking about. "Tell me more."

Alstan pursed his lips, and Alric knew he recognized his bluff. Luckily, his brother also knew not to embarrass his family in a public place, but that didn't mean he wouldn't have fun with it.

"He's coming back tomorrow," Alstan said at last. "You should come by and see how Father deals with him."

Alric had no clue what his brother was talking about but felt trapped. "What was the fellow's name again?" he asked.

Alstan smiled, "Lord Garig of Eastwood."

"From Mercenaria?"

Alstan leaned in close to whisper, "I've told you before, Alric, they call themselves Merceria now, have done for centuries. If you had spent as much time with your books as your sword, you'd know that."

Alric blushed. "Of course," he said, "but why would a Mercerian noble come to our court?"

"He wants to raise a rebellion against his king."

Alric snorted, "Father won't go for that."

"True," said Alstan, "but Father is wise enough not to dismiss him out of hand. He told him to come back tomorrow. He wants to hear his story in private."

"And by private, you mean..."

"With his advisors, of course, the usual bunch."

"So you, as his heir, will be there."

"Precisely," said Alstan, a smile crossing his face, "but I think you should be there too. It'll do you good."

Alric was not sure it would be a positive experience, but he had buried himself in his rush to avoid the young lady, and now he was committed.

"Besides," said Alstan, interrupting his thoughts, "Lord Weldridge will be there."

Alric's eyes lit up, "Uncle Edwin?"

"Yes, and I believe he just might have a seat for you at the tourney."

Alric smiled; a day at the jousts was just what he needed. He heard soft footsteps approaching from behind, but now his mood was joyous at the thought of tomorrow's activities. He wheeled about suddenly to face a startled Lady Julianne.

"Lady Julianne," he said, bowing deeply, "what a pleasant surprise. May I have the honour of this dance?"

He took her hand as she looked on in surprise, and led her to the dance floor; Uncle Edwin always said it was best to take the bull by the horns.

King Leofric of Weldwyn sat on a chair at the head of the table as Alric and Alstan entered. The king's eyebrows rose when he saw his youngest son.

"Alric? Are you ill?"

It was Alstan who spoke up, "No, Father, I thought he might benefit by coming. Shall I send him away?"

"No," responded the king, "it's good he's here. He'll give me another perspective. Come and sit beside me," he said, indicating the seats to his left. "Lord Weldridge will be here shortly, and then we'll let our visitor in."

They sat down and waited while the servants brought wine. Before they could pour, the king interrupted them, "I'll do that. Leave us."

After the servants left, Leofric turned to his sons, "Listen, but don't interrupt. You may ask questions if you like, but don't accuse and don't comment. We'll feel him out, see what he really wants."

Alric thought the whole affair was probably going to be a waste of time but nodded his head dutifully. The door opened to admit Lord Weldridge.

"Edwin," said the king, "good of you to come."

"Thank you, Sire, it was gracious of you to invite me. And what do we have here, do my eyes deceive me? Two Princes of the Realm?"

Alric blushed. It was all an act, he knew, and yet he was always glad to see his lordship. Lord Edwin Weldridge was not related by blood, but he may as well have been. He was the lifetime friend of the king, and to the rest of the family, he was simply Uncle Edwin, except, of course, at official functions.

"To what," Edwin said, glancing at the two young men, "do I owe the pleasure of such grand company?"

King Leofric spoke, "Alstan thought it might do Alric some good, learning the ways of court and such."

"Hmm," said Lord Weldridge, "I suspect it's a bit more than that, but perhaps that's a discussion for another day." He looked to the king, "What do we know of this fellow we're about to see?"

Other than his mother, Alric had only ever seen Uncle Edwin talk so informally to the king.

"The fellow who's coming to see us is a noble from Merceria."

"Merceria, you say? Anyone I might have heard of?"

"I doubt it; a man named Lord Garig. He's a minor noble, but he comes representing the Earl of Eastwood. What do you know of this earl?"

Weldridge pursed his lips as he often did when thinking. "I believe he's a very powerful man, Leofric, perhaps one of the most powerful men in their kingdom. We'd best listen carefully to what his representative has to say rather than dismiss him out of turn. Are we sure this isn't some type of trick?"

The king smiled, "I knew you'd say something like that. I've had the Steward of the Heralds check his documents. The seals are legitimate, as far as we can tell."

"Well then," said Weldridge, "let's get the man in here and see what he has to say."

King Leofric called out the order, and the door swung open, revealing a middle-aged man with a plump belly and a shortage of hair atop of his head. He stepped forward, bending his knee as he bowed.

"Your Majesty," he said, "I bring you greetings from the Earl of Eastwood."

"Please, Lord Garig, arise. Come, sit down, have some wine. We have plenty of time to discuss matters."

The man took a seat at the end of the table while servants rushed in to provide him with wine. Alric noticed that the maid, Lerna, was serving; the Royal Family had trusted her for years. She would remain during the discussion to look after them, and her excellent memory could be counted on for an accurate account of the dealings.

"Now, Lord, tell us what has brought you to our court," encouraged Lord Weldridge.

The Mercerian took a small sip of wine. "Thank you, Lord. I have the esteemed pleasure to offer you the chance to deal with a... let's say, problem, that has been plaguing your border for years." The man looked at the faces around him as he spoke, trying to draw them into his speech.

"What problem might that be?" asked Alric.

"Yes, please," said the king, "do explain, my youngest son is not familiar with the politics of Merceria."

Lord Garig smiled and nodded at Alric. To Alric's mind, the man looked like a serpent preparing to strike, but he sat still and listened, heeding his father's earlier words.

"There has oft been trouble between Merceria and Westland," the man started.

"Westland?" asked Alric.

Alstan leaned close to him and whispered, "That's what they call Weldwyn."

"Why Westland?" asked Alric, still confused.

"Think about it for a moment, Alric. Honestly, sometimes you can be as thick as a post."

The king's glare quieted the elder brother. Alric, finally understanding the name, nodded to himself, pleased with his conclusion.

Lord Garig, who had waited while the two brothers were whispering, now continued, "As I was saying, there has oft been trouble between our two kingdoms and it is known that the court of... Weldwyn would prefer to have a friendly neighbour. The Earl of Eastwood is proposing just such an arrangement."

"I see," contemplated the king, "and what would the earl want in return for this friendship?"

The man took a sip of his wine. Alric watched him closely, realizing he was trying to build courage for his next statement.

"His Lordship would wish you to support his claim to the throne."

There was silence at the table as the words sank in.

"I was not aware," said the king at last, "that the position of King of Merceria was available."

"Strictly speaking, it is not," agreed Lord Garig, "but King Andred is unpopular, and the people demand someone more... reasonable."

King Leofric nodded in understanding, "I see. Please tell me Lord Garig, what sort of support would the earl require?"

"Troops, Your Majesty, to ensure a... smooth transition of power."

Alric observed the neck muscles tightening on his father's throat; this suddenly had become very interesting.

"Let me get this straight," King Leofric clarified, "you would like us to send soldiers into Merceria to support the earl's bid for power. Is that correct?"

Lord Garig sat back, and Alric recognized an obvious look of triumph on the man's face. Little did he know what was about to happen.

"Precisely," the visitor agreed.

King Leofric looked to Lord Weldridge and raised his eyebrows. Uncle Edwin looked back, and as their eyes met, the king simply nodded, ever so slightly.

"Tell me," said Lord Weldridge, "what do you think would happen if a foreign army invaded Merceria?"

"Why, the people would flock to their side, my lord," said the Mercerian.

"I doubt it. Instead, they would unite in defense against a foreign invasion, and then both Merceria and Weldwyn would be embroiled in a war."

Alric watched his father as he stood, looking squarely at the man.

"I will not support this endeavour," he stated. "Weldwyn and Merceria have never been friends, but to act against your lawful king is treason, and I will have no part of it. You will leave our kingdom immediately."

The man opened his mouth to speak, but Lord Weldridge stood alongside King Leofric, "I think it's time you left. Alstan? Alric? Perhaps you would escort his lordship from the chambers?"

Alric sprang from his seat at the unexpected mention of his name. So taken by surprise was he that he banged his knee on the table as he stood. He tried to be stoic and ignore the pain, following his brother, only to limp as he went.

Lord Garig, for his part, kept calm, leaving the chamber to meet his own retinue outside.

Alric and Alstan watched the man depart; no doubt he would cause trouble elsewhere, but his time in Weldwyn was done.

∿

Continue the adventure in Heir to the Crown: Book 3 Heart of the Crown, now available at your favourite retailer.

A few words from Paul

The Heir to the Crown series is taking on a life of its own. The world has its own history and even events long in the past have had an effect on the story. The characters have extensive backgrounds, and I wanted to share some of these tales without detracting from the main storyline. I have collected an assortment here, in *Mercerian Tales: Stories of the Past*. Some of these stories answer questions, like why Albreda helped relieve the siege of Bodden. Others offer insight into the motivations and history of secondary characters, like Dame Hayley. If you are waiting for *Heir to the Crown: Book 3, Heart of the Crown*, fear not, it is being written even as this book goes to press. In addition, Book 4 also exists in outline form, and I will begin writing it shortly.

As with the other books in the series, I have many people to thank for their part in bringing these stories to life. Christie Kramberger, who continues to take the thoughts from my head and make them into amazing covers. My beta readers who patiently wait for the next chapter so they can help shape the story into what it has become: Brad Aitken, Stuart Rae, Andrea Kenny, Nancy Wolf, Amanda Bennett, Laurie Bratscher and Stephanie Sandrock. Thank you also to Brad Aitken, Jeff Parker and Stephen Brown for bringing the characters of Revi, Arnim, and Jack to life.

Above all I need to thank my wife, Carol Bennett who acted as Editor, Marketer and Social Media expert. You continue to inspire me to write and I love that we are on this journey together.

Finally, I must also thank you, my readers. My desire to write this book started as just wanting to put metaphorical pen to paper, but now it has become so much more. You inspire me to think beyond the walls of Merceria and create a larger world where all things are possible. Each time I receive a review, good or not, (I do prefer the good ones though), it has me thinking how can I make the series better. I use your input to fuel my writing, especially on those days that I am tired and just want to relax after working at my day job. Please take a moment and post a review to let me know which was your favourite tale from *Heir to the Crown: Book 2.5, Mercerian Tales: Stories of the Past*.

About the Author

Paul Bennett emerged into this world in Maidstone, Kent, England at the beginning of the 60's, then immigrated to Southwestern Ontario with his family six years later. In his teen years, Paul discovered military models, leading him to serve in the Canadian Armed Forces. Around the same time, he was introduced to role-playing games in the form of Dungeons & Dragons (D & D). What attracted him to this new hobby was the creativity it required; the need to create realms, worlds and adventures that pull the gamers into his stories.

In his 30's, Paul started to dabble in creating his own role-playing system, using the Peninsular War in Portugal as his backdrop. His regular gaming group were willing victims, er, participants in helping to play test the new system. A few years later he took his role-playing system and added additional settings; including Science Fiction, Post-Apocalyptic, World War II, and the all-important Fantasy Realm.

The beginnings of Servant to the Crown originated three years ago when he began a new fantasy campaign. For the world of Merceria, he ran his adventures like a TV show; with seasons that each had twelve episodes, and an overarching plot. After the campaign ended, he was inspired to sit down to write his first novel. He knew all the characters, what they had to accomplish, what needed to happen to move the plot along. 123,000 words later, Servant of the Crown was written!

Paul has mapped out a whole series of books in the land of Merceria and is looking forward to sharing them all with his readers over the next few years.

CPSIA information can be obtained
at www.ICGtesting.com
Printed in the USA
LVHW040824070719
623349LV00004B/537

9 781775 335511